The Bench

The Bench

Kusum Ansal

Vitasta
Let Knowledge Spread

Published by
Renu Kaul Verma
Vitasta Publishing Pvt Ltd
2/15, Ansari Road, Daryaganj,
New Delhi - 110 002
info@vitastapublishing.com

ISBN 978-93-86473-20-2

Typeset & Cover Design by Vitasta Publishing Pvt Ltd
Printed by Vikas Computer and Printers

Preface

All of us are aware that death is an absolute reality of a human life. But we don't give much attention to it, as life has its manifold attractions which keep us lured and we live in their enchantments. But sometimes during the journey of life suddenly one reaches a point where one stands face to face with death. A total vacuum, *shunya*, a dark alley of suffocating silence, which crushes one's physical, mental or materialistic desires. That strong stillness prevails all around, the stillness of time between life and death.

My novel deals with the experience of that particular time. My main character, Natasha, is a barely thirty-year-old woman, who started her life as a student of psychology, and went on to achieve a doctorate and make a meaningful career out of it. But in between, as it happens with most of the young girls, she gets married.

After two or three years of a blissful married life her husband Shailendra meets with a fatal accident. Struggling with pain and numbness in his injured body, he is forced to be in a hospital bed for more than a year. Natasha's dreams of a bright future shatter, as time brings her face to face with death.

During that time, Natasha sits on a wrought iron bench, day and night, in the hospital corridor, watching her beloved Shailendra decaying every day. Under the circumstances, sitting on the bench Natasha could have become a lifeless iron statue herself...but instead she reacts positively and tries to make full use of that difficult time. She comes across many incidents, personalities, variety of human relationships, common people of different religions, medical experiments etc. They all implant a deep and living faith, a self-faith in her, totally based on her mature inner intuitions. That phase of her life reconstructs her entire mental and physical space. She achieves the unassailable self-confidence of a complete and independent person. She even reaches a step up to welcome death, the final goal of life...liberation and realization of the truth or reality of life.

Dr (Mrs) Kusum Ansal

'What will you do today, beti?'

'Hmm?' I turned around startled. Vidyawati ji had held out a cup of tea for me. I took it gratefully and sipped it in silence, maybe because so far I had not considered the question at all. What would I do now indeed?

She stood there, her question still unanswered.

'So...where is Papaji?' I asked.

'He has left, beta. Some friend of his came over from the college to accompany him.'

'Oh, I didn't know...he didn't say anything before leaving.'

'No, you should also dress and leave for office, child. How long will you grieve like this?' She patted my shoulder with unusual warmth.

Yes, I had to take stock of the situation now—get up and think about what I needed to do. Up to this moment I had not even tried. Which fuel could I use to light up a fire that would guide my way? My lamp had always been short of oil. How could I blame the storm?

It was true. I had to pull myself together... after such a

devastating quake... I shivered. The memory shook me up again. But no. This turbulence rose from emotion. I had to rise above all this and focus on consciousness. Slowly, I knew I had to come out of the fear of my dreams crashing down and employ myself in rebuilding my life. I had to find the way.

At that moment the newspaper boy dropped the newspaper at our doorstep and vanished. The recent events had shaken me to the core. Indeed, I needed to wake up. Because the newspaper was a reminder of the present...of events in the here-and-now, it would lead the way.

As I picked up the newspaper, I noticed the veranda floor sodden with dirt like Time past. The stubborn layers would need to be scrubbed away with water. The same layers of dust and grime seemed to have settled inside me too. I had ignored them for so long. Was this really in my nature? No! This couldn't be me.

In front of the veranda there was a little patch of vegetation that had grown into a garden. Papaji had been trying his best to add some more greenery to it. He had painstakingly removed the dry twigs and bushes and planted a row of plants that remained green regardless of the season. Some of them had flowered. In the middle of the bed was a Gulmohar tree laden with red flowers. Papaji had taken care to build a cement enclosure around it. One could sit comfortably on it. The most attractive feature was the path made of old blue tiles that connected the veranda to the enclosure. Some words were written in a different script with pictures on the tiles. Papaji had mentioned they were china tiles he had bought from a kabadiwala. I didn't know what a 'pagoda' meant. But he explained the tiles were a part of Chinese handicraft. The pagoda was a place of worship for Chinese people. Exhibiting their culture, these tiles were an important experience that enhanced our garden. Perhaps they reflected the broken pieces within me, the feeling of being crushed.

A little squirrel ran helter-skelter around me, climbing up and down the tree again and again. Sometimes she would pause to nibble the food in her hands, wag her tail and break the stony silence around. She was a symbol of life that seemed to be slipping from my hands. Suddenly, I felt the need to sit down. I needed some stability beneath my feet. I found the old bench Papaji usually sat on very inviting. It was an emotional moment. It created the same feeling within me that the hospital bench inspired. I felt a deep bond with the inanimate structure.

If you come to think of it, one's life is filled with so many quakes that it is killing. If I turn around and try to figure them out, I realize that people's emotions are not deliberate constructs. Nor are they our own creation. They just happen as a natural phenomenon. They are what sets each person apart from the other as a unique individual. And it is a person's emotions that grant them the courage and ability to change the course of their lives. As I did. My research. My work. Marriage with Shailendra.

My research in the field of Psychology had revealed that human beings were the only species who not only had consciousness, but also emotional quotient. Then why did I find myself floundering? I needed to find my feet and deal with the altered circumstances. Why was I still struggling?

Several years ago when I joined the university to study Psychology, the sole aim of my life was to become a great psychologist. But today life had brought me to this point where I felt a greater need for faith and prayer. I needed something to ease the pain—some logical reasoning, cure or healing ingredient.

As I was leaving, Vidyawati ji said, 'Beta, there is no fruit at home. Do bring some on your way back. What about your lunch?'

'I will come back and eat. Maybe dal chawal. Make something...anything. What fruits should I get?'

'Whatever you like...whatever Bhaisaab likes. Yes, he likes pomegranate.'

Once I was outside the gate, I paused and stared at the house, as if acquainting myself with it all over again. I had been so preoccupied with the hospital, rushing in and out, that I had never really noticed anything. I had been so obsessed with my own thoughts that nothing else was visible.

It was an old house in the middle of an open ground. Two of its bedrooms, a veranda and a bathroom belonged to us. I had not even bothered to find out who lived in the other rooms. The board over the gate read 'No 50, Hastings Road'. Underneath, a dilapidated nameplate had 'Ved Prakash Mehra' embossed on it.

Warren Hastings. Some foreign official, antagonistic to the freedom struggle, linking us to the East India Company?

Forget it. My sentiments were useless.

But that historical wide road was quite busy, jam-packed with fast cars, bicycles and pedestrians. A few makeshift shops stood next to the rickshaw stand. They stocked vegetables, fruits, soap, oil and other materials of everyday use. Good, I thought. I would buy the things I needed on my way back.

I was just about to sit in a rickshaw when a beggar on crutches stopped me. Frightened, I quickly opened my purse, took out a ten rupee note and handed it to him. 'Oh...'The pain within reached my lips. It would have been so difficult for me to see Shailendra in that situation.... Even Papaji, for that matter, was not doing a very good job of it. As long as he was alive, Shailendra had struggled with pain. That is why Papaji, initially, in his worry, sold off everything to build his son's future, and later this house—to save his life.

At that moment another beggar came and stood near me, held out his bowl and said, 'Give me something, daughter.

May your children and husband live long ... God bless you....'

I was piqued. He didn't know what he was saying.

'Go! Go away!'I shouted. 'I don't have anything.'

Couldn't he see the emptiness inside me? But he dragged himself beside the rickshaw as we began to move. Eventually, I had to give him ten rupees to get rid of him. I had no coins in my purse. The moment I reached the hospital, Harry would make me drop some change in his 'donation box'. And I always obliged.

'You have reached your destination, madam.' The rickshaw puller broke my reverie.

'Really? Have I reached? Where...?' I was at the main entrance gate of the hospital that defined and would perhaps symbolically govern the rest of my life.

I was paying the rickshaw puller when my phone rang. It was Mandira.

'How are you, Natasha?' she enquired. 'Haven't seen you for a couple of days. Zafar is here these days. All of us friends would like to meet you. If you can, you must come along with us in the evening...for old times' sake! Tell me what time you can make it. I'll inform the others. And I'll come and pick you up.'

'Mandira, I've just returned to the clinic after a month's absence. I don't know how many patients I have or how much time they will take. I cannot say, but I'll call you. Okay, Mandira.'

I disconnected abruptly and rushed to my cabin. I bumped into Harry on the way. 'Oh, Natasha! Good to see you.' He almost hugged me.

Sister Dorothy, Elena, Dheera surrounded me. Before they could speak up, Harry said, 'Please don't utter platitudes. No grieving, okay?'

Still, Sister Dorothy came up to me and kissed my forehead. 'Be brave, my child,' she said. I knew she had unshed tears in her eyes. Before any one of the others could utter a word or mention Shailendra's name, Harry caught me by the hand and led me to my cabin.

'Come on, start your work,' he said. 'Let me get you some coffee.'

It seemed he was in greater need of sympathy than I was. I could still feel myself tremble and settled down upon the chair. Yet my mind kept returning to Mandira's words. Little do we realize where life takes us as unsuspecting observers. Sometimes, suddenly, we just find ourselves in life-changing situations or circumstances that later play a huge role in our lives.

I was just about to sit down at the table when my phone rang once again.

'Hello, Natasha?'

'Yes, Papaji.'

'I called home. Vidya Behen told me you had left for the hospital. Good you did. Be brave my child. I'm there always whenever you need me.'

There was deep silence on either end of the telephone—as though words had drowned somewhere, in some unimaginable abyss. His words echoed in my ears: 'I'm there....' Whose duty was it really? His—or mine?

Papaji ambled through the tunnel of memories and parked himself at the other end. And I found myself thinking of the days at the university when my entire being was filled with ecstasy. In the Psychology lab, 'Sir'—Mr Ved Mehra was explaining dreams to us and doing an interpretation of those dreams. Saumitro Sir also had a class on character and character analysis. He was explaining traits, descriptions, special features. I had to collect all the material and prepare a presentation. When the discussion began, Sir Mehra said, 'Natasha, why don't you come over to my home this evening? I have some great books on the subject; you can borrow them. They'll be of immense help.'

He scribbled his address on a piece of paper. 'Karam Bhoomi'.

In the evening I took a rickshaw to reach the address. When I arrived I saw a huge building with the name he had scribbled on the chit he gave me. There was a guard at the gate who stopped me. 'Yes, madam, whom do you want to meet?'

'Does Mr Ved Prakash Mehra live here?'

'Yes, the Professor sahib? You may go inside. Ask anyone in the office; they will call him.'

'Alright. Thank you.'

Inside there was a small lobby. A few chairs rested against its walls. Pictures of some saints hung above them. A few women snored on the chairs. As I walked in, they stirred to look at me. Their eyes were expressionless. The mere act of observing seemed a chore for them. A puzzling inability was frozen in those eyes.

A middle-aged man stepped out of the office.

'Yes, madam?'

'I'm looking for Professor Ved Prakash Mehra.'

'Yes, he lives on the first floor...on the left. Wait.' He turned to another door and called out, 'Vidyawati.'

'Coming.'

A woman in a white saree, with her head covered by the pallu, walked up to me gracefully.

'Listen, Vidyawati, take this young woman to Professor Sahib's room. She is his student.'

I took the elevator to reach the floor above. By this time I had realized that it was an old people's home. Most of the residents, exhausted with age, considered it their permanent base. Maybe some of them had no children, or if they did, the children did not care about the existence of their parents any more. When the elevator stopped, a sour-looking fellow rushed inside.

'Rajinder? Did you meet Dadi? She remembers you day and night,' said Vidyawati.

'None of your business... I've deposited the cash for the month and I've bought her some clothes. How does it matter whether I meet her or not?' He pushed her aside and left.

She turned to me, 'See, beta, his grandmother has been living here for seven years. In her initial days she used to talk so much. She would pick up a quarrel with anyone she could find. But she was the one who taught me to read the *Ramayana*. Apparently, when she was young she used to be a well-known schoolteacher somewhere. Last year, her son dies of cancer. Ever since then she has turned into a stone. She has given up picking fights. She doesn't accuse anyone of anything anymore. Her son left her here and now this grandson comes to pay for her every month. See there she is. He didn't even greet her. But she calls his name, 'Rajinder', day and night. She yearns for her family, yearns for someone to share and care, but no, there is nobody in the whole world. If I don't encourage her to get up from her bed, she would stay on it forever. I bathe her and make her eat.'

I noticed sitting right in front of me a shadow of a woman. She sat like a statue, staring at the ceiling, oblivious to the world around her, probably lost in some memory from the past. I tried to recall the term we use for such a state in Psychology. I was sure I would find several interesting case histories at this Home.

Right then the door opened and 'Sir' stepped out.

'Oh, Natasha. Come, come. Do come in. I was waiting for you.' He turned to the woman behind me. 'Vidyawati ji, please could you send two cups of tea?'

'Of course, Bhaisaab,' she replied and left, but I could still feel her voice and inhale her scent.

It was much more than an ordinary room and it certainly belonged to an extraordinary man. The four walls were packed with wooden shelves. Big, heavy books filled most of these racks. It was easy to associate the professor with them. Only the wall right opposite me had an open window. A study table was placed against it. An assortment of files and loose paper lay upon it. Outside the sun was setting. I don't know why the sight of the fading light created a strange sense of melancholy in me. I could feel some indescribable churning within, but could not explain it. It could not be defined; simply experienced.

I spent some time with him discussing the topic and he explained the nuances. At the end when I rose to leave with the books he had offered, I could only revere the man in front of me. Psychology taught us that this reverence or faith was the essential ingredient for learning, for developing one's character. It was crucial to imbibe knowledge. As I left, this sentiment accompanied me, and I knew it had come to stay.

We were at the party room at *Simran* celebrating Alka's birthday. Popular music played in the background. We were lost in a world of our own. Music has a unique impact upon our psyche. Suddenly, at some distance from the window I noticed Professor Mehra sitting at a table. There was a young man with him, perhaps a student. I wondered if he was another student like me, seeking help from him for a research project. But I usually sought his help at the old people's home. Though I never mentioned it to him, I was strongly influenced by his personality and intelligence. I always tried to converse with him whenever I got an opportunity. My own parents and relatives at home were barely literate. Besides, I was researching emotions—the state of mind of a person, sense of self, consciousness and sentiments; my topic wasn't easy. Working with Professor Mehra I discovered the vast canvas of his mind and realized that analyzing one's life was not a simple task.

I stood up and walked up to his table. 'Hello, Sir,' I greeted him. 'You...here? I've never seen you here before.'

'Hello Natasha. Yes, this is the first time I've come,' he said. 'Come, meet my son. This is Shailendra. He has just graduated from IIT... Shailendra, this is Natasha....'

'Hello.'

'Hi, good that you managed to persuade Sir to step out of that smoke infested room,' I said. 'I'm so happy to see him here. Honestly, even after having achieved so much he lives the life of a hermit...so detached. Thanks.' As I looked at the young man's face, I felt a strange shiver of excitement.

'But Sir,' I continued, 'You have such a grown up son? It's amazing. You look so young! Perhaps thanks to your yoga classes?'

Somewhat embarrassed, Professor Mehra was still mumbling introductions. 'Thanks. Natasha...Shailendra; Natasha is doing her research under me. She is an outstanding student. And Natasha, Shailendra is going to join a very prestigious bank soon.'

'Oh, all the best.'

'May I ask you a question, Natashaji...? You have spent a lot of time with my father. I have come for a visit after almost a year. Is it just me or do you too feel that he has become too quiet, that he seems to be withdrawing into some kind of a shell?' His voice choked with emotion.

'May be this silence is a prerequisite for personal liberation,' I said. 'And frankly, I don't think Sir is shrivelling in any way; I think he's being enriched by his experiences— like some meditating sage. His students are very impressed with him. In fact, the whole college considers him a genius. We all respect him.'

'Perhaps. But somehow I cannot bear his silence.'

'You know, I am researching human emotions—their variety and variations—and silence is the culmination of so many of them. Silence is the answer to many questions.'

'It's possible that you guys feel that way. But I'm quite worried. Ever since I've come I've been noticing that he doesn't even sleep properly. I got the mattresses changed, even the duvets and pillows, but it hasn't changed anything.' He slipped into past memories.

The professor took his hand and pressed it hard. 'You know how it is, Shailedra. There is frequent change of guard in my life. Of course I've dreamt of sweet slumber many times, but never been able to make it mine. But now that you're here, we'll have our own home and I'll be able to sleep in peace.'

Shailendra studied his father carefully, as though observing a stranger.

'Home....'

Perhaps he could see signs of life emerging in his father. Maybe he wasn't just a lifeless sculpture any longer. Right in front of us he was changing into a flesh and blood person he once was.

I don't know why but Shailendra suddenly put his hand over mine on the table. Perhaps he was so preoccupied that he did not think.

'Natasha ji, my father believes in you, in your intelligence. And even I'm impressed with you...the way you analyze everything? Your voice too is hypnotic.' He settled his gaze upon me. 'Natasha, I would like you to become a part of our life. Please...we'll have a home. My father will be able to sleep.'

The whole situation had suddenly transformed into a scene out of a film. I was shocked and leapt to my feet.

'What—what do you mean? What are you asking?' I was incredulous.

All of us stared at each other. His words hung in the air. What a ridiculous request it was. We stood rooted to the spot for a few minutes as though frozen by our thoughts.

My fingers were still laced with Shailendra's. Before I could move, Professor Mehra put his hand over ours.

'Please Natsha,'he said, 'I don't think Shailendra can find a better life partner than you. I have full faith in your abilities. Your humanness and simplicity has always impressed me.'

'Sir...' I did not know what to say. It was surreal. 'I don't even know him. And what about my research—my future?'

Myriad thoughts raced through my mind. Both father and son continued to stare at me.

It was true Shailendra was Professor Mehra's son, but to me he was still a complete stranger. There were so many images floating in my head, but they were still unfamiliar territory. I didn't know how to paste them on the blank notebook that my life was.

Trembling, I raised my eyes to the window. Outside the sunrays were receding, leaving a mist behind them. Dry yellow leaves scattered in the wind. They seemed out of sync with the turbulence I was experiencing.

I did not know what or whom to believe. Should I believe in these new relationships that had been unexpectedly thrust upon me? This young man's decision could change my life forever. It could create a whole new world for me.

'Happy Birthday to you. Hey Natasha, come, Alka is about the cut the cake,' Mandira's voice reached my ears, bringing me back to the real world.

But Shailendra's grip over my hand was still firm. He did not really need to convince me. I stole a glance at him. I had never seen such eyes—deep, black and trusting. His persona was as powerful as his father's. His impeccable clothes did not seem to fit in the surroundings. When he bent forward, I could smell the cologne on his body. So far I had not met a man who used perfume on his body. Trying to release my fingers, I wondered how I could define this bizarre feeling.

As I left the chair, I could feel Professor Mehra's sharp gaze on me. It gave me the same excitement as a lecture on a thought provoking or interesting subject in class.

'Please, Natasha. Think about it, beta,' he said.

'Beta'...once again, a plea to the vulnerable human side of me I could not easily ignore. He patted my head with his tremulous hand. Touch has its own language.

'Sir, how do I categorize this incident?' I spoke up. 'The possibility of emotion...or its impossibility.'

'Natasha, please transfer this incident—our request—from the realm of abstract theory to real life.' The professor's hand still rested on my head. 'Be practical, because I'm serious. I've thought this over very carefully.'

Shailendra's deep black eyes had an expression I could not read.

Near the window on the wall opposite hung a picture of Guru Nanak. His palm was raised in a blessing. It gave me some solace, as though reassuring me. I don't know, but there must have been some celestial vibrations at play. Staring at that poster Hermann Hesse's *Siddhartha*, the book I had recently read, came to mind. The protagonist of the novel, Siddhartha, lived near a river. He spent many years of his life sailing on the boat from one end to the other. He not only observed the changing face of the river from time to time, but internalized the changes himself—sometimes calm, sometimes turbulent, sometimes restive like a youth, and sometimes, as in the summer months, thirsty and dying like an old man. It was like the journey of life. Eventually, it reached a point where all the worldly activities ended. The banks became blurred. Only tranquility remained. Siddhartha could imbibe this serenity from the river. He had been witness to the changes year after year. The experience had brought him from curiosity to a comfortable kind of stillness, plucked him away from the false ideologies of previous lives lived. He knew the sweet reward of sacrifice.

Similarly, the image of Guru Nanak dangling on the wall of this restaurant was a witness to whatever was transpiring within its four walls. He was a divine witness to these crucial moments of my life. Could I call it a 'proposal'?

'Oh Madam Philosopher, come, Alka is about to cut the cake!'

Manjula was dragging me away now. How was she supposed to know what had happened in these few minutes I was absent? From those precious moments, the budding new relationships, I was suddenly transported to the here and now, the real world hustle-bustle of the restaurant. I was stunned. And preoccupied. I could still feel Shailendra's fingers interlocked with mine. I could still sense the Professor's palm upon my head in blessing. I could still feel the blinding light exuded by the portrait of the living legend on the wall across from me. My mind was in turmoil. And in the background the friends began to sing, unaware of the sweeping changes in my life. This was life.

Very few events in life really count as being very significant. Our convocation ceremony was one such. Alka and Sarika had bought themelves similar sarees, white with a deep red border. The MA students had to wear the red border ones, while the BA ones had to wear a blue border. I had already worn the blue bordered saree two years ago.

As is always the case, the chief guest arrived late. But Shailendra had arrived on time, with Professor Ved Prakash Mehra. My mother too had come with Urvashi and was sitting in one of the back rows. A little later my father too arrived in an ordinary and rather soiled pyjama kurta that made me cringe. Perhaps he had come directly from the shop.

The convocation ceremony began. The principal wore a black gown and a black cap with a long silky tassel. The chief guest was similarly dressed. It was a pleasant atmosphere. The programme began with a Saraswati vandana followed by a short speech. I don't know why, but Shailendra's presence would not allow me to relax. I was trembling within, though I could not understand why.

The principal's words rang out, 'Sir, by virtue of the authority vested in me, I present you these ladies and gentlemen who have qualified for the award of degree of....'

All of us stood up. It was time to receive our degrees.

The chief guest said, 'I confer upon you the degree of Master's and expect you to be worthy of the same. I also ordain you to wear these robes as the insignia of the said degree....'

Our black robes were symbolic of the degrees we were being awarded. Each of us stepped on the dais, received the degree from the chief guest, shook hands with him and plastered smiles upon our faces for the camera. Shailendra had also stood up to click pictures of me with his mobile phone. Somehow it created a turmoil inside me. After the ceremony we stepped out in a jubilant mood. Amma, Baba, Mandira embraced me. Professor Mehra and Shailendra too approached me and said, 'Congratulations, Natasha.'

'Thank you, Sir. You haven't met my parents....' I thought this would be the best time.

'Oh, congratulations to you too. Your daughter is very talented. She has written so many academic papers recently, some of which I have sent to a university in the US. I'm sure they'll be awarded.' He stepped closer to my father.

I don't know how much of it my parents understood, but Baba said, 'Our little imp has been mad about books right from the beginning. She just wants to study. I thought, since we were illiterate and uneducated, at least one of us would do well to study. That's why we got her admitted to an expensive school. She used to win awards there too. What was she...?'

'The head girl.' Urvashi spoke up. 'My elder sister always gave me a complex.'

'Yes, even now she's won a medal for scoring the highest marks,' said Sir.

'My sister, Urvashi, is doing BA Hons in literature,' I said.

'And this is my son, Shailendra.' Sir proudly pushed him forward for introductions.

Before we could say anything, Alka, Sonika and Mandira turned up.

'Oh, you're here. Let's go, Natasha. The photographer's here.'

Shailendra invited me for dinner that day; he wanted to celebrate my convocation. Except for the *Simran* I had never been to any hotel. Nor had anyone invited me out like this. I could only confide in Mandira. When I told her about Shailendra, she leapt up.

'Arrey, Natasha...you're lucky! Really lucky. It's a good offer. After all, you have to marry someone...I saw him on Alka's birthday...how he held on to your hand....If such a decent guy has proposed to you, you mustn't let the opportunity go. Just grab it.'

Like me, she was overwhelmed by the circumstances.

'I was wondering why you have been so quiet lately. All through the convocation you were preoccupied; you hardly smiled.'

'I'm in a dilemma, Mandira. Tell me what to do. You know how I love my books. I just wanted to finish my project and become a professor. You are a witness. Have I ever looked at a guy? And then, Mandira...what about the love between you and Zafar?'

'Yes, there is a big question mark on our relationship.

My father is not ready to accept that I want to marry a Muslim boy. And I cannot live without him. Love, Natasha, is a very strong emotion. It ties two people together. And nothing counts but that bond—not religion, not society, nothing....'

'But I have never been in love. I have never thought about it.'

'Fine. Start thinking now. Raise your eyes from the books and look at the real world around you. Learn to live in it. And, Natasha, be practical. You belong to an ordinary family, an ordinary environment. Even if you become a professor, what will you achieve? Students, library, practicals—the same cycle over and over until boredom sets in. This marriage will change your life. You will get a chance to travel—to step out not just from this city but maybe the country. You may be able to see the world. I was telling Zafar I'm tired too. If possible, we should go abroad—maybe to Paris or someplace. What's there to keep us here, in this little town?'

'There is the Taj Mahal.'

'That lover of yours—he'll construct a new Taj Mahal for you. His bank job will take you beyond the Taj Mahal to see the world. I can already see a bright new future. Okay, you have to dine with him tonight, don't you? Show me what you plan to wear.'

Mandira arranged my hair. I rummaged through

Amma's sarees and picked out one. Mandira brought some make up from her house and applied it on my face. I was unacquainted with this new woman who stared at me from the mirror.

Stepping out of the taxi I entered a beautiful hall. The environment was completely new for me. I stood amazed, my feet trembling, barely able to support my frame. Several tables stood covered with spotless white table cloths. On top there were bouquet arrangements of various kinds. I had never seen such flowers in my life. It was as though music swept through the room, carrying a fragrance in its arms. A sense of mystery lingered in the air. I felt ill at ease, uncomfortable in my clothes—in the saree. Suddenly I stopped.

'Shall we go somewhere else?'

'Why, what's wrong? Come, sit.' Shailendra took my hand and made me sit down on a chair. There was a strange sensitivity in his manner. And in my mind there was restlessness and curiosity.

A waiter came and stood next to us.

'What would you like to drink, Natasha?'

'What—whatever you like. I don't know. What do people drink in this restaurant?'

Shailendra laughed. 'Coke or lemon juice?'

'Lemon juice.'

Shailendra placed the order for both of us. Free from these duties he said, 'Okay, Natasha, I want to know you. Tell me about yourself.'

'Me? What do I say?' I stuttered. 'I really don't know anything about the business of living in the real world. I live in an ordinary home. You have met my parents; they are simple and middle class. That is how we are. I only wanted to study, so went on with it. I have'nt made any plans or mapped a destiny for myself. After my Master's, I'm doing research under your father's guidance. I thought I might be a professor after my PhD. But then I don't know where you suddenly appeared from to....'

'To decode you or to create you?'

'I don't know. At the moment I'm just looking for the ground to plant my feet firmly on. Please tell me, what did you see in me that made you...?'

'I don't know. I honestly don't know what came over me that day.'

The waiter brought our food. The two glasses of lemon juice were chilled enough to send a shiver down my spine.

'Cheers,' he said, and raised his glass in the air. I had seen this kind of performance in the movies.

'Cheers,' I lifted mine in an imitation of him.

The glasses clinked and something in my consciousness stirred.

It was difficult for me to eat with knife and fork, but I watched him and tried to copy his actions. These mannerisms, this sophistication was entirely new to me.

He said, 'Natasha, I studied at Mayo College in Ajmer where mostly children from royal families come for their education. In that environment there is a special focus on manners and etiquette. You may find mine a little different, but don't worry. Both of us will change some.'

There was a deep sincerity in his eyes. Had he firmed up his decision already? But didn't both of us stand at two different ends of a certain culture?

'Yes, let me tell you ... when I saw you for the first time, in that restaurant, you seemed a different kind of woman—innocent and pure. But there was something about your eyes, an attraction, like that of dark grey clouds, and then, of course, Papaji mentioned your intelligence. After that external appearances or looks did not matter anyway.'

'Still...there's a huge difference between us. At best, I'm from a more than ordinary lower middle class background. How can you take such a major decision of your life just like that? I think you should reconsider. You cannot live your life based on a moment's decision or on impulse. We need to be realistic. We are two strangers who have just met. I don't know anything about you. Yes, I know Sir. I know about his life at the old people's home. I meet him there for my project sometimes.'

'Yes.... All right, let me open a few old pages from the book of my life in front of you today. My father, mother—we lived in a narrow street in Agra. I think the name was Mython. We had a house there. I was born there. Papaji's elder brother and his wife lived in a house next door. My mother belonged to a rich family. She was also very beautiful. Maybe that's why the atmosphere—the squalor and grime in the drains, the garbage dumps, the stinky and stale air proved too much for her to take....'

Meanwhile, the waiter had served our food. Both of us began to eat slowly. Shailendra sipped the water now and again, perhaps to wash down the unpalatable events of the past.

'My mother never held me in her arms affectionately, Natasha,' he continued. 'My parents fought night and day. You know what my father is like—brooding, wise, a visionary....I'm sure he must have been good looking too in his time. He must have had to bear so much. Perhaps his research helped his transfiguration and transformation. Else, my mother's rejection of him could have made him go insane. But he spent most of his time in libraries, amongst books...learning, teaching. He did not fall apart, but instead was determined to reach for the stars.'

He took my hands in his. I noticed tears at the corners of his eyes.

'Natasha, I used to observe that my father often went

to bed hungry. Sometimes, he would hide in a corner of the house and weep. Then one day Ma took me to a school in Ajmer and got me admitted. She sold off everything she had—jewellery etc. to pay the fee for five years. She wanted me to study in a good school and become a successful man, not like Papaji. Then, one day, without saying a word to Papaji, she disappeared. Ranjan Mama told us she had left for London. Papaji gave our house in Mython on rent and went to live in the staff quarters. He was also sick of the daily bickering of my Taiji. He spent his entire earnings to build a future for me.'

I don't know how long we sat in deathly silence, finishing our food.

'Ice cream...yes, we must have ice cream. It's important to prevent the burning inside the stomach .... When I came down last time, Papaji praised you a lot. For the first time I felt that he had noticed something apart from his books. He had removed the veil of frustration from his eyes momentarily and raised them to the sky. He seemed alive after a long time.'

'Oh, I know nothing about that! I don't know what he thought about me...or whether he is right....'

'Maybe after many years he saw a good woman—someone who could fill his hollow wilderness of a life with colour.'

His gaze held myriad emotions; trust, love, fortitude.

'But I didn't do anything for him. Yes, I used to sit and talk to him a lot. Perhaps because I found him very different from my own uneducated family. He was very graceful. I might as well tell you—there is no sophistication or finesse in our family. We are simple, straightforward people. Whatever I have learnt, I have learnt from my friends...and books. Just once, a group of three or four girls, including me, went to Delhi with Professor Neelima. I have only seen Delhi. And I saw knives and forks for the first time at the guesthouse where we stayed. That kind of style and elegance was beyond my imagination. In that fashionable world I saw Kafka's play, *Metamorphosis*. The whole experience was amazing. It was sort of a transformative process, a new beginning in my life.'

'Me too, Natasha. I learnt all the major lessons of my life at the hostel of Mayo College. Initially I had an inferiority complex, but slowly I came out of my cocoon. I started scoring better marks than anyone else in the exams. Many awards and academic achievement paved a way for me in the world. I became a favourite with everyone.'

'A favourite with women too?'

'Maybe. Girls did find me attractive. Every day, on my seat, I used to find a piece of paper smelling of roses or jasmine, with Urdu poetry on it. But strangely, whenever I wanted to pay attention to a girl or extend a hand in friendship, I was held back by a deep sense of pain and loss in the shape of my mother. It overpowered my consciousness.'

'Oh...really?'

'Yes, Natasha. I would go to the gym, wear boxing gloves and vent my frustration on the boxing bag with full force. I would hit it again and again till I was spent and the smoke had evaporated from within. My fingers would writhe in pain.'

For the first time I felt something stir in my heart. I grasped both his hands with mine.

'Please stop thinking about the past now. Don't think about it anymore. Please, Shailendra.'

It was the first time I had called him by name.

I wondered about his mother and about how deeply she must have hurt his feelings while he was still a young, vulnerable child. His pain and open wounds had still not healed.

'Tell me,' I said, 'didn't you ever feel like meeting your mother again or getting to know her? A mother is a mother after all.... Didn't she try to keep in touch?'

'Natasha, all my school reports and exam results used to go to her. I had even taken her London address and phone number from the college register. Many a time I was tempted to call her, but never did. My father's wilted face always prevented me. He used to say, "Shailendra, never allow a woman the right to destroy you completely: not only your character and personality, but your very will to live. Yes, she did me one favour. She left you here for me. And thanks to that I have forgiven her from the bottom of my heart."'

Perhaps it was a dream—a sudden, unexpected twist of fate. A piece of paper with a government seal and 'court marriage' on top made me Shailendra's wife. On the insistence of my parents we had performed a small ceremony at home, according to the Arya Samaj rituals, with the holy fire as our witness. I liked the customs, the scent of henna on my palms, and the feeling his fingers putting vermillion in the parting on my hair gave me. The ambience had a divine touch. My own body felt alien; there were so many unfamiliar currents flowing through it. And there he stood, the architect of the entire process, 'Sir' who was now 'Papaji' for me too.

Papaji had now created a house. He had waved a white flag to his life. He was now busy fulfilling a lifelong dream. Now that he had his own place, he would often be found with the *mali* in our garden, discussing new plants and caring for the new pots and beds.

Meanwhile, he had also brought Vidyawati ji from the old age home. She helped us in setting up the kitchen, utensils, tables and chairs so that after some time the house shaped up as home. He called me and said, 'Natasha, this is Vidyawati ji. She's not a servant but is like a sister to me. Give her respect and affection; she has been through a lot in life.'

'Ji Papaji.' I bent and touched her feet.

'Oh Bhaiji... you're too kind....' The old woman wiped a tear with the end of her pallu and embraced me. 'Bless you, beta. Stay happy always. May your husband live long.'

'Shailendra and I are leaving for my mother's house. Why don't you come with us?'

'No, you go. I'll accompany you some other time. Meanwhile I'll finish cooking.'

Amma, Baba and Urvashi packed a great deal of stuff for me to take back and got it loaded in the car. Hidden from everybody's eyes, Amma tied a black thread around my neck. 'Beta, this is a blessing from a very well known Pir Baba. Never remove it. Now you have such a good household, family, husband ... this will ward off the evil eye.... It will protect you.'

'Amma, please....'

'Come, you make a fuss every time. Listen to me this once. Don't take it off.'

Shailendra arrived to pick me up. I could feel my old life—Amma, Baba, Urvashi—slipping away, while on the other end Shailendra stood welcoming, with a thousand hopes in his eyes.

As we were sitting in the car, he said, 'Natasha, come to

think of it, your name is quite modern. Who thought of it?'

'Nobody. You know, when Amma took me to school for admission, the student seated on the chair in front of me told me her name was Natasha. I found it very appealing—even mysterious. When my turn came, I gave my name as Natasha. Amma was quite upset. She said, "What are you doing, girl? Your name is Gayatri." But I replied, "Amma, from today it's Natasha and nothing else."'

'Oh, no wonder. This name probably belongs to a heroine in a Boris Pasternak novel—it has that Russian flavour. Strange that someone with a foreign name like that should walk into my life.'

'Really? I didn't know. I was so busy with my own thesis that I never found the time to read literature. Still, I watched some films based on the classics, such as *Dr Zhivago* or Victor Hugo's *Les Miserables* and even read a few novels. I wanted to understand the Russian revolution and the Nazi cruelties. I wanted to understand the psychology behind intimidation and the various aspects of humanity—masochism, communal despair, discontent and thirst for blood.

'Natasha, please forget your Psychology and Russian Revolution for a moment. Let's talk about lust. Talk about Lady Chatterley. He touched my lips with his fingers and avoiding the driver's eye, showered my hand with kisses. 'I'm familiar with the Urdu poetry of Ajmer too, that flows like a sweet fountain in my heart....Everything will be forgotten... our truths or lies...once the sun goes down in the ocean that is your eyes.'

I too was overcome with emotion. I sat, lost in the poetry of his words, staring at him.

'Say something, Natasha.'

'What do I say? Such pretty lines....I've never heard such poetry....'

This was a period of transition. What was I experiencing? What a sea change. Suddenly, I wanted to shower everything I had upon him.

'Natasha, tell me, how many times have you seen the Taj Mahal?'

'A couple of times. Maybe three or four, I'm not sure. I haven't been there for a few years since there was work pressure.'

'Come then, let's go today. In any case it's a full moon night. Let's experience the symbol of love together in the soft moonlight. Let's see this imposing structure—the height of Shah Jahan's love. All lovers seem to develop a complex before this magnificence.'

'Will you be able to love me like that, Shailendra? I've heard Mumtaz Mahal was very beautiful...and I...I'm just such an ordinary woman....'

'Come on, you always underestimate yourself. Or maybe it's because you're honest, and therefore humble and soft spoken. And that is what I like about you. Natasha. I discerned all those qualities in you that I wanted in my life partner. And then, am I any Shehenshah? I'm no Shah Jahan, mind. Just a young man from a broken family.'

'Oh, don't be emotional, Shailendra. You're quite a handsome man. Perhaps you have your mother's genes. I heard she too is very good looking. But thank God you only look like her and do not behave like her.'

'Do not think about it, Natasha. Let's not dig up the painful memories Papaji and I buried in the graveyard of our past long ago. Come, let's hold hands and walk on the road to love and trust. We'll see the glorious dome of the Taj Mahal shimmering in the cool moonlight.'

We stood on the marble platform, mesmerized. Our whole being was overwhelmed by the sheer beauty of the building.

The guide had the facts by rote—the entire timeline of history, the splendor and opulence of the Mughals. But I had lost myself in the spectacular round dome that drew me further into myself. It was an unmatched experience. I leaned my head against Shailendra's shoulder and was almost swept away by a wave of contentment.

The guide's voice brought me back to reality now and

again. 'Look carefully, dear guests, this Taj Mahal—the greatest symbol of love between Shehenshah and Mumtaz Mahal—is actally a tomb. And yet it seems as though it's a dreamer's cozy nest on earth. Look at the dome studded with semi-precious stones. They glitter like stars, sometimes bright, sometimes dim.'

'No. I feel the moon's rays are talking to the dome and humming a tune, a romantic song. And that melodic strain has parked itself over my ear like a pretty earring.'

'Let me tell you another thing, Madam,' said the guide. 'Whenever it rains, a droplet of water falls on Begum Mumtaz Mahal's grave. Nobody knows how it gets there. It's a gift of sadness—perhaps the grief Shah Jahan kept locked inside himself for so long after her death. The droplet is a symbol of the misery that finds a vent every year. It's an expression of the sorrow of separation.'

'Oh, it's true that separation is killing.' Shailendra pulled me into a tight embrace. Our breaths intertwined in perfect rhythm; our bodies yearned for each other, prodded by the full moon. Shailendra had closed his eyes. After bidding goodbye to the guide we sat there for a long time, lost in love as it were, with delight in my heart and absolute bliss in my trembling body.

Shailendra seemed to be groping for words. Suddenly he stood up and said, 'Seriously, Natasha, it was a special moment when you entered my life. My life was all turmoil, but you are the solid rock that holds it together now. I will always live in you. You will give me refuge, won't you?'

Words such as these, the dreamlike quality of the situation were still too new for me. I felt numb. It seemed like the scent from Amma's incense sticks that she burnt in front of her Gods and the light of the diyas she lit in the pooja room every morning, had pervaded my life. Was I really alive, really living this dream?

'Kiss me,' I said, offering my trembling lips to him. In the next few minutes the sights and sounds around were lost to us dissolved in our bodies.

Inside the dome there were two graves close to each other, with flowers and leaves all over them, as though two bodies lay asleep, in a tight embrace.

'Do you know, Natasha, Shan Jahan deliberately left space for himself near Mumtaz Mahal's grave. It was his wish to be buried there upon his death.'

'For sure they must have reunited under the folds of the earth even after death. Their bodies must be lying against each other, overcome with love.'

'Yes, in that darkness I'm sure there must be light—their smiles buried somewhere underneath.'

'The very idea of separating to reunite is kind of fantastic, isn't it, Natasha?'

Preparations were on for our trip to Singapore. Papaji watched the hustle-bustle on his way in or out. The light seemed to have gone out of his eyes. At times, defeated, he would sit down on the bench in the garden. Those days some renovation work was also going on in that garden. Papaji had bought some old blue Chinese tiles from a kabadiwala. He wanted the path, from a particular tree inside a cemented enclosure to the house, to be paved with them. Each tile had artistic etchings in blue. Some showed pagodas; others had Chinese writing upon them. Indeed, they looked very pretty laid between patches of grass, almost as if a blue stream was flowing in between the greenery—that too deep and attractive. I was tempted to keep sitting there staring at it... they imparted a strange energy or a message.

That morning when I came out of the room, I noticed that Papaji, who sat at the dining table every day dipping his biscuits in a cup of tea, was absent. The emptiness of his chair disturbed me.

'Oh...Papaji...where is he? Vidyawati ji...Papaji...?'

'He's sitting outside,' she said, handing me his tea tray. 'Take it to him, dear.'

When I stepped outside I saw him sitting quietly in the garden. He seemed preoccupied.

'Oh...Papaji...why are you sitting here like this? Are you all right?' I touched his feet and then checked his forehead. 'No fever I hope...You leave for a walk so early in the morning.

Maybe you've caught a chill.'

'No, no beta, I'm fine. In fact, I didn't even go for a walk today. Just didn't feel like it.'

'Then?'

'Oh...so many questions have no answers, Natasha. Come...sit down.'

'Okay.' I went and sat down beside him. 'Papaji, where did you get these tiles from? They have brightened up the whole lawn. It looks as if they have their own identity and history—as if they want to rise up from the porcelain and say something.'

'So you too feel like that, eh? Really? I was going somewhere with Saumitra in his car. He stopped at the Kabaadi Bazar; he wanted to buy something. And suddenly my eyes fell on these tiles at a shop right in front of me. The seller was busy washing them in a tub. He would take each one out, wipe it and put it out to dry. I don't know why I sensed a mystery hidden in them, as if the words on them wanted to say something. For some inexplicable reason they drew me to them and I bought them. In any case, antiques are valuable, aren't they?'

'Yes...and you've got them laid out very nicely. They look like a brook flowing through our lawn.'

'And the pagodas and the letters? Doesn't it seem as if they've gathered together to tell us that identity or intimacy of a family is indivisible, unbroken?'

'Or maybe that our destination is our journey... I mean the pagoda. And the seeker is seeking himself.'

'Great, Natasha. I like your interpretation.'

Vidyawatiji arrived with her tea. There was a packet in her hand wrapped in a faded cloth. She handed it to Papaji and said, 'Bhaiji, I've brought it.'

'Yes, give it to me, Sister,' he said. Taking it from her he passed it to me. 'Here, this is for you.'

With trembling hands he undid the white cloth packet and piled the sarees on my open palms.

'These are Kamini's,' he said. 'She was very fond of good clothes. When she left, there were too many of her things left behind, but I only brought a couple of these. Now you keep them. Wear them if possible.'

He had mentioned Ma's name for the very first time. It was a significant relationship—their bond, despite everything—unbreakable yet invisible. However, in our house it was the first time that her name had been uttered at all. No matter what they say, some family members never go anywhere even when they are gone. Their memories remain in their special place in our lives. They're there in our every breath. Each word we speak has a soul and life. Perhaps that is why when I felt the slippery silk in my hands, an image had already begun to form in my head. For a while Papaji and I sat silently, as though enveloped by a strange shadow. The sarees...Ma...Kamini—the words seemed to have taken up shape in the air amidst us.

'Beta Natasha, these are old, but they have Kamini's sweet scent, her touch. I hope you didn't mind...'

'Oh Papaji, only a few minutes ago you said antiques are invaluable, didn't you? Then of course these are like blessings for me. To tell you the truth, Papaji, I've never seen such expensive, such gorgeous sarees ever before. Honestly.'

I put the sarees against my forehead for a few seconds. They seemed to give me immense pleasure. As if they hid something deep and meaningful—maybe a sign. It had no language, but I could sense a depth, a kind of waiting, femininity. As though one was seeking oneself. Where had I lost myself?

'Papaji, you have never mentioned anything about Ma. Please tell me what she was like. Prashant mentioned she is very good looking.'

'Yes, Natasha. Kamini's beauty is unmatched. Her father had a huge family; they were very well-off. They had respect, esteem...everything. It was wonderful. But her father died of a heart attack following a sudden, unexpected loss in business. Kamini has an older sister. She married a Christian boy and moved abroad. Those days her brother used to be my student. I had just become a professor. Upon his insistence Mr Ranjan got me married to Kamini. Perhaps she did not want to marry. She came from a huge mansion. Staying in a two room, less than ordinary house in the godforsaken street of Mython became a huge challenge for her. It was a culture shock too. Even though I tried some alterations, the house could never be good enough for her. A stinky drain ran right in front of it. In the corner there was a little temple. There were kirtans, crowds, constant noise—none of which she could swallow. They were unbearable for her to live with.'

'But Papaji, you're so handsome. You're no less than anyone. All the girls used to admire you in college. And so many years ago, it must've been even better...?' And your love and dedication? How about that?'

'Yes, Kamini did try to adjust initially. At that point I couldn't give her much time. I was preparing for MPhil. Even my financial status was pretty weak. I used to earn very little those days. On top of that, Shailendra was born within our first year of marriage. It took away all cheerfulness from her. Her beauty faded somewhat since the body suffered changes. Though I tried my best to console her, she held him responsible I think; she could never really love him. I started offering tuitions and employed a maid for her, so at least she could leave Shailendra at home and step out.

'Sometimes, in the absence of a maid, I would stay behind at home to look after him. I would cook and feed him. My elder brother and Bhabhi lived next door, but Bhabhi was always taunting us. Her barbs and misbehavior cut us deep.'

'Oh Papaji...you had to go through a lot. I'm sorry...I didn't know....'

'Yes, child. The worst part was that Kamini considered my nature and the pursuit of my studies foolish.'

He seemed to be slipping into the abyss of past memories.

'I still remember—whenever I returned from college she would say, "Is this life? My husband returns home and what does he bring in his bag? A load of homework, student's notebooks...a broken body bent over the computer.... This whole atmosphere is disgusting. I cannot live here." Sometimes she would say, "To fan one's husband while he's eating is an outdated practice. That he should finish eating and wipe his hands with the pallu of his wife's cotton saree. This cannot be my idea of happiness or romance, Ved. I'm sorry. I'm not cut out of that mould. And I cannot act for too long. I feel suffocated in this house. Keep your slave culture to yourself." Sometimes she would shake Shailendra in frustration and say, "What is this kid turning into? That little school at the corner of the street—what options will it be able to offer him, Ved? Do you ever read the newspaper properly? Do you know where the world is going? Do you know what development is? Let him be a man, not a blackboard—a black slab on which his fate is marked. At least set him free." '

'Then one fine day, overwhelmed with her anger, she ignored my struggle-ridden austere life, my studies, tuitions —and vanished. In the seven years of our marriage, the chasm between us had grown. When I returned home from college, the maid did not tell me anything, but Sona Bhabhi's words still assault my ears like molten glass. "Brother, your wife turned out to be not just any diamond but the Kohinoor. She's become a memsaab. I hear she's hooked up with some really big fashion designer. You ignored everything...and now she's even taken you son."

'I was very upset for some days, but then I received a letter from Kamini. She informed me that she had got Shailendra admitted to Mayo College in Ajmer. Mayo College—where the children of royal families and the rich and famous studied. He would stay in the hostel and manage to get somewhere... become a decent human being. She had also written that she had sold off her jewellery and deposited his fee for five years. That gave me enough time to arrange for his higher studies.

'In the dark skies overhead I suddenly spotted the Pole Star. Suddenly I felt revived. I overcame a heart attack and went to meet Shailendra. I felt assured that he was in good hands. Things were taking shape in a way I had never even imagined. And Natasha—for this incredible gift I forgave Kamini from the bottom of my heart then and there.

'Natasha ... today is her birthday too...."

'Papaji, you don't have any photograph of hers in the house. Why?'

'Kamini either took all her photographs with her, including our wedding album, or destroyed them... I don't know....'

'Oh...'

I went looking for Vidyawatiji.

'You aren't up yet today. What's wrong?'

'Beta, I have a bad body ache. The moment I try to rise from the bed, my head starts spinning.'

'Oh, did you take some medicine?'

'No...I ran out of it a long time ago....'

'Oh, please tell me the name, I'll get it for you. Until then let me apply some balm on your back...'

'Let it be, beta....'

Vidyawatiji's face was pale with agony. Even though she resisted, I went into Papaji's room to fetch the medicine. His diary lay on the table, as though he had been writing something before he stepped out. He was supposed to leave for a seminar. This thick, soiled notebook lying open didn't look like something that had notes of Psychology in it. I returned with the balm in my hand, but the notebook had made me curious. Did Papaji write a diary?

In spite of Vidyawatiji's protestations I rubbed the balm on her back, wrapped a blanket around her and brought her tea.

'Come, finish this tea and lie down. You must not exert yourself. I'll just get your medicine, some fruits and vegetables. You can have some biscuits in the meanwhile.'

'I'll get up and make something in a bit. Bhaiji likes gobhi parathas; maybe I'll make them. Don't trouble yourself. You've just got married; you shouldn't worry about these minor things. Yes, send someone to get something for Shailendra if you have to.'

'No, no, I'll buy everything myself. Just tell me the name of the medicine.'

I left for the market. The chemist was not too far. Neither was the vegetable vendor. Upon returning home I went straight into the kitchen and grated the gobhi to make the parathas for Papaji. Then I made two toasts for Vidyawatiji. When I entered her room, she was sitting with a small suitcase lying open in front of her. The room smelt of poppy or rose—probably a spray she had used to rid herself of the smell of lodex. She had pulled out a printed saree and was touching it to her forehead as if it were some holy book. Her face shone in the dim light of the room.

'Here, have a toast with your tablet. The pain will disappear soon.'

She began to eat in silence.

'Are you going somewhere? This suitcase...'

'Yes, beta. Today is the 24th, isn't it? On the 24th of every month I go to the railway station.'

'Really? But why? You never mentioned. And I never noticed either. Anyway, do take your medicine.'

I handed her the tablet and the glass of water.

'You shouldn't love me so much, beta. People who love me tend to leave me. Some depart from the world. I'm most unfortunate. Don't know at what inauspicious hour I was born.'

'Ah, but I'm not going anywhere. Come on, finish your toast while I get my coffee. Then you can tell me why you go to the station on the 24th of every month.'

Once I returned I said, 'Alright, now tell me, Vidyawati ji—now I'm free. It's only four o'clock. Shailendra will come around six.'

'I've never told anyone...Bhaiji knows a little. But if you really wish to know, I'll tell you. Where do I begin the whole saga...?'

God alone knows what and how much she swallowed along with her tablet.

'My life was like a desert, beta. I must have been twelve or thirteen when I was married off. I had no mother. My father got it done at an age when I didn't even know what marriage was. By the time I became conscious of it, a tall, strong man was squashing and scrunching my body like dough. If I resisted or cried, he would hit me. Then night and day I would slog in the house. I worked like a machine, oblivious to all pain. I became a lifeless statue. I was uneducated, so I had no idea how many years I spent in that situation.'

She seemed to slip into some dark by lanes of the past. Then she swallowed her boiling hot tea in one gulp. The machine had found the fuel. A page that spoke of her pain from the annals of history lay open before her.

'Then—then do you know what the bastard did? He said, "You, bitch—you're barren. Get out of the house! Come on, pick up your luggage and I'll drop you at your parents." I couldn't say anything. I had no voice in that house. I could only groan. I had become dumb. I had never stepped out of the house. I was like a prisoner.'

I went up to her and propped her trembling body against the bed. The skies of the memory dimmed and brightened at will. Her face was covered with sweat; her veins seemed to be choked with thorns. I stood up and wiped her with a towel. But it seemed as though she was elsewhere.

'So, beta, we sat in a train and left. I was happy that I was going back to my father...but it was not to be. I don't know what city it was, or which station. I just followed him. And the house where we finally landed up was not my father's. When he knocked, a bearded dirty-looking man stepped out and took us inside. He said, "You rest; I'll just come."

"But this is not my father's house. Where have you brought me?" I asked.

His hand flew and struck my cheek. "You talk a lot, don't you, bitch!" he spat.

'The bearded man made me sit down on the bed and brought some breakfast. "Eat," he said. "I'll take you there in the evening." But beta, afternoon turned into evening and evening into night, but my husband did not return. Several days passed. The bearded man informed me that he had bought me. My husband had sold me off for three thousand rupees. Can you imagine—me a sold object. Humans aren't sold. I was just a piece of dead wood....I don't know where I was going. Only that single room was witness to my agony. The bearded fellow and his friends would grind me night and day. I would lie bloodied for days. Man's lust makes him a monster. I could not count. God knows for how many months I endured that hell. In fact, that life was worse than hell.'

Listening to the story of her helplessness and slavery made me feel sick. She had never let on in so many months that she had been through such trauma. Vidywatiji was silent now. Maybe memories of the knotty past inside were bubbling over. The smell of iodex was thick in the air, but the veins continued to ache.

'Then one day Ramnaresh appeared. I don't know if he was the servant of the house or what. Morning and evening he would unlock the door to my room and give me food and water. Sometimes he would bring in soap, a towel and new clothes. Maybe because he saw me soaked in blood. Or in a semi-conscious state. But beta, he never touched me. Nor did he ever speak. Then one day he appeared in my room at night, opened the door and said, "Here, Sister, wear these clothes and come. Let me set you free from this dungeon. I cannot bear to see your condition any more. Today Prakash Saab has gone out; he'll be back in two days. It's a good opportunity. Quickly, get dressed." My mind was numb. I had lost the ability to think or feel. I bathed and wore the clean clothes. There was no mirror in the room or the bathroom. I don't know for how long I had not seen my own face. My identity was lost even for myself.'

'Oh, does this really happen in the world?' I was stunned. 'Vidywati ji, your life was a real torture.'

She was wiping the sweat on her face like someone who has just become conscious of her body.

'Then what happened, Vidyawatiji?' I had unconsciously wandered into her past.

'This cruel molestation and mutilation of the body—is it a never ending story? Doesn't the law do anything? Is there no punishment?'

'Yes, beta—there is everything. The keepers of the law know everything, but they too are men. Hungry bastards. They don't bother with penalty.'

For a while the two of us sat in silence holding each other's hands. It was becoming difficult to breathe in that air.

'So, we climbed into a train quickly. He got something to eat and drink. Even he was as nervous as I was. But he said, "I know a lady in Agra, Panno Bibi. I have informed her; she'll be there at the station to receive you. Just leave with her and don't look back. I'll take the returning train." I saw his face clearly for the first time. Yes, there are still some good human beings in the world. I wanted to trust him. By then the station arrived. Bhai Ramnaresh took my hand and helped me down. That platform almost became a place of worship for me—the zone between two worlds. An imposing lady stood in front of me. Ramnaresh introduced me to her and said, "Panno Bibi, this woman has suffered a lot. She was kept locked in a room by wretched demons for four months. I managed to rescue her with great difficulty." '

"So should we report him to the police?" she said.

"No, Behenji. He is a powerful man and very well connected. I think you should just give her a new lease of life."

'He quickly climbed into the train that was leaving again. I stood like a stone, unable to even thank him. We left the premises soon enough too. Panno Bibi took me home. The next day a picture of him appeared in the local newspaper. He had jumped in front of a train and committed suicide...but Natasha, I know it wasn't suicide. I'm sure one of Prakash Babu's henchmen must have pushed him in front of a running train. It was the 24th. I still have that day's newspaper. He was like an angel for me, beta. He had literally liberated me from hell.'

Once again we sat in deep silence. We had no words.

'What happened next? Vidyawatiji, your life is a saga—a

novel. I am flabbergasted. How did you endure so much?'

'Sometimes you have to, beta. It also happens to people who could never imagine such a thing happening to them. Like Panno Bibi. She had a good size bungalow and she lived alone. Her son and daughter lived abroad. I lived with her peacefully for about two years. I used to look after her; cook and clean for her. Then her son and daughter-in-law came back. They sold off the house and the rest of the property. They put Panno Bibi in an old age home and me along with her. That was where I met Bhaiji. Panno Bibi was very attached to her house. She could not bear the heartlessness of her own children and cruelty of her fate and died within six months. Bhaiji and the other occupants helped me with the last rites. Her son and his wife never even turned up for the ceremony.'

'Oh really?'

'Yes, beta, such is life. You find both heaven and hell on this earth. And people like Ramnaresh—who actually laid his life down for my sake. Even in the Home, there were some very nice people. There I learnt to read and write from scratch. Mrs Mohan taught me how to read the *Ramayana*. That's it. My mind was filled with light. Now I have Bhaiji—and you—and a son like Shailendra. My life is complete. May God bless you. Now I must leave. I have to make an offering of flowers at the station. It's like a temple for me—my pilgrimage.'

'Yes, you must. But please take a rickshaw. And do get some more vegetables when you come. Shailendra has invited some people over for dinner tomorrow.'

'Alright, don't worry. I'll manage everything.'

She changed into another saree, took the little basket of flowers and left, but her scent still hung in the air in her room. Amma used to say we Hindus have thirty-three crore gods out of which she prayed to Lord Krishna. It was a symbolic number...countable. But today, I felt every human heart had one, his or her own, like Vidyawatiji's... the 24th...Ramnaresh...the railway platform....

'Hey Ved, good that you invited us. It's a decent house you have here. There are even flowers in the garden.' He looked at me.

'Come in, come in, Saumitro. This is my son, Shailendra ... and of course you already know Natasha.'

'Oh Natasha, so you married him? And such a handsome man too. I'm happy for you...Where were you until now, beta? Never saw you before.' He took Shailendra's hand.

'Sir, I was at Mayo, Ajmer, initially—and later at IIT Kanpur. I hardly ever got time to travel home.'

'He would have come had there been a home,' said Balvir Sir, coming in. 'God knows in which old age home this wretched Ved decided to stay.'

'Please have some,' I offered the tray to them. 'Lime juice or squash?'

'Oh yes.' Balvirji lifted a glass. But Saumitro Sir pulled out a little bottle from the pocket of his kurta. 'Don't mind, Ved Babu, but I knew there would be no drinks served here. That's why I brought my own bottle. Listen, beta, please give me an empty glass and some ice.'

'Sure.' Shailendra brought everything he needed.

'It was a good move, Ved, to shift into this place. That old age home—I don't know how you managed to survive there. Aloneness and loneliness—you must have suffered both. You were already alone, and in that crowd, you became a hermit. Living there your isolation was growing so much that it was apparent in your personality.'

'Yes, true. I was living there at an age when I shouldn't have been there. And I went about the business of living too, since living is an essential part of life.'

'Forget all that. Let bygones be bygones. Now the times have changed for you.'

'Not really, Balvir. Sometimes it happens that some knots linger in your mind. It becomes difficult to gauge how to prioritize yourself. That was another reason why the Home made sense. The crowd was good and the place was clean and neat. Their emotional study was important. The Home was a constant reminder of their deep rejection and depression.

Their own children had dumped them there—for whatever reason. And that too at an age when they needed love, care and support the most. They had such expectations from life—but they found only desolation. Memories in lonely times were a constant reminder that they were still alive. But there was an emotional vacuum that never left them. I got to experience so many different things.'

'Okay...the different experiences must have been enriching.'

'Oh Natasha...you look so gorgeous in this saree! And Shailendra, this kurta pyjama really suits you. Great.' Mandira's laughter echoed in the room, lightening the atmosphere. She hugged me affectionately.

'Come, meet my friend, Zafar. Zafar, this is my childhood friend, Natasha...and this is her husband, Shailendra. And this is Ved Sir....'

Zafar stepped forward and offered a kind of salaam. His hand touched his forehead; he bent a little. He was dressed in a white salwar and a full-sleeved kurta. A Muslim cent per cent. All guests seem to freeze for a second. Zafar's presence, the scent of his perfume in the air seemed a little out of place in the house.

'Welcome, Mandira. Come in, Zafar Bhai. What would you like to have?' I served them the beverages. He helped himself to a glass of the green squash, brought it close to his eyes observing it and said, 'Thanks.' He had a powerful voice.

'Welcome, Mandira. Seeing you after ages.'

'Yes, Sir. I was in Delhi for a few days.' Then she caught Shailendra's hand and said, 'Zafar is an artist, Shailendra. He's spent most of his life in Paris. I met him last year at the art fair in Delhi.'

'Oh great. So Zafar Bhai, are you holding some exhibition here in Agra? Which gallery?' Shailendra shook his hand.

Zafar was fair. He had a broad forehead; long, wavy brown hair, and a chiselled body. He looked like a work of art himself.

'No, no, I didn't come here for any exhibition; I'm here to see old monuments and the tombs of old sultans. It's a city of Mughal culture. The air itself has a classic touch to it. This city has an unusual soul—and that fascinates me. In front of every tomb, every temple or mosque I stand and admire their craftsmenship. Hats off to the craftsmen. What amazing architecture.'

'Yes, the history of this place makes one nostalgic. And not just history but also the intricate carvings of the shrines.'

'You're right. I had never even imagined that there would be such beauty here. Every artisan has displayed such detailing of his work: flowers, leaves, nature—I mean, nothing is out of proportion. Nature seems so alive and fresh even in stone...as if every plant can breathe; every tree can shed leaves, or bear fruit.'

'And then the foundation stones of the monuments, the building material is soaked with the water of love, Zafar Bhai. Buried love combined with the earth washes one's being.' Shailendra took my hand.

'Have you painted anything since you've come?' It was becoming difficult to maintain a natural flow of conversation.

'No, Natasha. I've just been doing a little bit of sketching, that's all. My paintings are in a studio in Delhi. You should come and take a look. I'll be glad if you do.'

'Yes, sure.'

Suddenly I realized there was no picture or paintings on any wall in our house. Not even an artwork. Or any photograph. All the walls were blank—bare, breathing a silent air.

'Oh...would you like a drink?'

'No, Sir, thank you. Where will I find this sherbet again? And then this too is a part of the culture of this place. Its colour, its sweet smell, it's intoxicating, just the ideal thing for a restless artist like me.'

'Yes, these days artists are so much in demand. Paintings are so expensive.'

'This is Saumitro Sir. He teaches us character—I mean Psychology,' Mandira told Zafar.

'Really....' Zafar seemed surprised.

'Cheers.' He raised his glass in the air.

'Cheers.' All of us raised our glasses too.

'Come, let's sit there.' Shailendra invited Zafar to the other end of the room.

'So you guys are leaving for Singapore I hear. That's what Mandira mentioned.'

'Yes. It's a bank job. You must come. And Mandira, you too remain in touch.'

'Of course I'll come. You're taking my friend along with you.'

'I'm also fond of journalism. I write on art for some newspapers. Don't know when I might land up there,' said Zafar.

Just then the door opened and Urvashi entered. She had some polythene bags in her hands.

'Sorry Didi, I got delayed. Couldn't find a rickshaw easily...'

I jumped to my feet. She was feeling awkward amongst so many people. Her salwar kurta too was quite ordinary.

'Urvashi, my sister,' I introduced her. 'Let me get the food served....' I took her inside. Amma had sent some food along with the *kachauris*. We laid the table. Everybody stood up.

'Oh wow, great food,' said Zafar.

'It's very simple vegetarian food, Zafar Bhai.'

'Oh, I've had such tasty 'parwal' only after Kolkata. Yaar Ved, this is brilliant.'

Saumitra Sir was enjoying his food.

Everybody sat down with their plates. Papaji looked quite

content. Gulab jamuns from *Simran* seemed to be the main source of pleasure. Vidyawatiji had also made kheer.

'Hey Natasha, a perfect evening,' said Balvirji, patting my shoulder. 'Thank you...and Ved, I am happy for you. Shailendra, Natasha is a bright girl. Take care of her.'

Everybody was laughing. They seemed happy. I was glad. It was like reinventing myself. I was playing a new role. A homemaker.

Urvashi brought something wrapped in a green leaf.

'Sorry, Didi. I forgot to give it before. Amma sent a jasmine gajra for you.'

A pleasant fragrance filled the air.

'Oh, how nice.' Shailendra took it in his hand.

'No, no...' Papaji's trembling hands snatched it away from Shailendra as if it were some repulsive insect. He said in a sharp voice, 'No, Natasha, you will not wear this gajra.' He flung it into a corner outside, threw a strange glance at Saumitro Sir and abruptly vanished inside.

There was deep silence. The soft scent of jasmine lingered, leaving its mark upon that evening.

Papaji had already bidden us farewell. Vidyawatiji had packed my belongings. Amma and Baba had also brought a great many things for me. Was it really eight months? I never realized it in this house. Time had flown as if by magic. Had I ever imagined it earlier? A part of my mind wanted to go to Singapore; another wanted to stay behind. The unwrinkling of Papaji's face to a great extent, his improving health, routine and financial affairs were important to me. Yet, I had to go.

Singapore too would add a new page to my life—a page filled with anticipation and ambition. The joy of experience flooded each atom of my body. Shailendra had led me to a seat on the plane, holding my hand. I was nervous and hesitant, but he gave me courage. And he was the one who tied my seat belt too.

Then he bent over and whispered in my ear, '*Chalo dildar chalo, chaand ke paar chalo....*'

I was staggered. I wanted the moment to feel real.

'How unromantic you are, Natasha,' he smiled.

'So what can I do to make myself appear romantic.'

'Sing the next line: *Hum hain tayaar chalo....*'

'Oh, how do I know? I haven't seen too many films. Nor did I get much time to listen to music.'

'Why do you always want to remain a student, madam? Now forget Psychology for a while and learn to enjoy real life, okay?'

'Okay.'

The airhostess brought something on a tray. Shailendra handed me a long glass with golden sparkling liquid in it.

'Champagne,' he said. 'When we celebrate an occasion we drink Champane. To new beginnings...and a new life ahead.'

He raised his glass. It clinked against mine.

I found the drink strange, sharp but sweet; it surged through my veins and gladdened my heart. The journey indeed wove a tapestry of dreams; it was a world beyond the clouds—it was sheer heaven. The plane landed at the Singapore airport. There were flowers everywhere in the city. I had been plucked from the city of the Taj Mahal and dropped into this wondrous land of dreams.

I would stand in front of the mirror and think—was I the same Natasha who, not very long ago, did not even have decent clothes to wear? I would wear anything Amma brought me stitched by 'Nanhe Darzi'. And here I was shopping for trousers and sweaters from Takashimaya, with Shailendra. The environment had changed...and so had I. In the evening, on the way home, Shailendra would often pick up flowers. He decorated them on the centre table himself, humming, '*Baharon phool barsao...*' and would kiss me with great passion.

I tried to comprehend his language as much as I could. He played music on the player. By the time I prepared the food, he would have our wine glasses filled. He breathed Hindi film music: '*Mujhe tum se mohabbat ho gayi hai... Mujhe palkon ki chaanv mein rehne do....*'

Sometimes he would put the wine glass to my lips and say, '*Yeh jaame mohabbat peene do....*'All this while the kitchen reeked of spices, the burner's flame, the roti on the tava—which often got burnt in the process.

And then I would say, 'See what your "*jaame–mohabbat*" has done now.'

His response was yet another song, '*Ud Ud ke kahegi raakh, sanam, yeh darde mohabbat sehne do.*'

Those words...the pieces on the chess board...overturned. Love...what kind of an emotion was it? Or sex as its culmination—two bodies rising, falling in sweet harmony. Bearing the pain was also a part of that love.

Then one day the telephone rang.

'An accident!'

I hailed a taxi and reached the address I had been hurriedly given. The scene before my eyes shattered my will to live. The unconscious, blood-soaked body of Shailendra was being lowered from an ambulance. The lips that were always humming cheerfully were covered with a plastic mask.

'Wha...what happened?' The sound of my own voice made me feel faint. I was all alone in an alien city. I called Papaji. I don't know how he mustered the strength and courage to travel all the way by himself. Somehow, together, we managed to have Shailendra transferred to a nursing home in Agra.

When the reports came in we discovered that a blood clot

had moved with the blood flow in his body and lodged itself in some part of his brain. Not only that, it had also affected the other veins. Some bones were broken. As a consequence, most of the right side of his body was paralyzed. Whenever Shailendra regained consciousness, he would scream with pain and then fall unconscious again. The pain was awful. The report we received from the hospital in Singapore said 'Necrosis' and a 'special case of dyslexia'.

I didn't even realize how the days passed. I would watch the needles, the plastic tubes slammed into his body with a glazed look. Some helped him breathe; others pumped glucose and medicines into his system. God knows what he was going through. He could not talk. If he tried, little bubbles would gather round his nostrils and mouth.

Papaji would look at me and I would look back at him—at his languishing condition. Each day was a burden. All the doctors in the hospital, especially Dr Sandeep and Dr Prashant, were trying their best. They said, 'Shailendra is stable now...maybe even out of danger. But it will take him a long time to recover. Let us see.'

He was shifted from the ICU into a room in the private ward. I would spend my entire day either in his room or in the corridor outside, seated on the bench.

The moment I arrived in hospital, I would open the door to Shailendra's room wide so that he could watch people come and go even from his bed. I did not want him to feel he had become a liability for us. One deadly accident could snatch away every little joy from one's life, make mincemeat of dreams and fling them on the hospital bed. Why did it have to happen? Why did it have to happen to me?

'Hi Natasha.' Shailendra waved his frail hand.

'Good morning, Shailendra. How are you? Did you sleep well?'

Before he could respond I pushed the music DVD in the player on the three-legged table and switched it on. His favourite ghazal.

'Gulon mein rang bhare vaade nau bahaar chale,
Chale bhi aao ki gulshan ka karobar chale.'

Mehdi Hassan's voice filled the room like mist. But for Shailendra, 'walking' was like a crime.

Where had my poor husband landed instead of in a garden (gulshan)? A garden needed fertile land. And for that natural beauty was essential; lush green grass, trees laden with flowers...but this hospital corridor...the room infested with the smell of medicines...couldn't be that. The tubes knocked into his body to help him breathe couldn't be butterflies. How could there be any creativity here—any lyricism or poetry? Only layer upon layer of agonized cries were pasted upon the white walls.

I didn't have the courage to look at Shailendra. Putting everything on the table, I quietly slipped outside. The bench there was safe. I sat down.

That day I had to prepare notes for my research experiment. I had returned to my previous work. Sitting on this bench was destiny. It was better to lose myrself in books rather than in misery. I had stumbled upon one by Sartre. I was reading a criticism of his philosophy. In *Being and Nothingness*, the idea of individual existence and individual essence was interesting. It said that when man loses his freedom and accepts collective values and rights, he becomes a thing.

So...sitting here in this narrow space in the hospital, with this suffocating smell of chloroform, had I turned into an object too? Where was the Natasha who had learnt to fly high in the sky? What had happened to her colourful dreams?

Sartre brought 'being for others' between my 'existence' and 'individuality'. It brought me face-to-face with a numbing revelation: a relationship between one's self and others was not possible. Even love did not offer anything except dilemmas and complications. No relationship allowed freedom. It was a lie that freedom was respected because the relationship itself defined the limits of that freedom.

What kind of a perspective was this? The question swam in my head. My freedom, my essence, my individuality defined not just Shailendra's life but mine too. Everything had gathered with me, into this little space, onto this little bench where I sat. Had we been married and fallen in love only for our life to turn into this bed of thorns? Slowly my situation was becoming clear. The whole atmosphere was bent upon my reification and I was exhausted, turning into stone. I felt like I was turning into an 'object'—what Sartre called 'non-being'.

If only I could lose my essence and melt in this bench on which I sat.

'Oh that's good, Natasha. Very nice to see you with a book. I like your attitude.' Dr Sandeep had just arrived for Shailendra's check-up.

'Thank you, Sir.' I followed him into the room.

Shailendra lay in the centre of the spotless white bed, growing paler every day. Sister Dorothy had already sponged him and changed his clothes. Perhaps she had also helped him shave.

Dr Sandeep removed his oxygen mask and said, 'Hello Shailendra. How are you? How do you feel today?'

'Don't know, Doctor. Maybe there isn't much improvement. More than half of my body has turned lifeless. Why isn't any medication working? What do you think?'

Dr Sandeep looked at his chart. Then he examined him with a stethoscope. Sister Dorothy had arrived by then.

'Good morning, Sir.'

'Good morning, sister. Did you give him the injection?'

'Yes, sir. I gave him all the medicines and the injection after breakfast. I also took his temperature. It just doesn't come down. Even now it's quite high.' She showed him the thermometer.

'Anyway, Shailendra, let's see. What else can we do? But let me tell you, you look quite handsome.'

Before Shailendra could reply, Dr Sandeep put the oxygen mask back over his face. There were several questions in Shalendra's eyes that he wanted to voice, but his hands were too weak to pull off the mask. Somehow Dr Sandeep managed to avoid them.

'Come, Natasha,' he said once we came out. 'Please step into my room for a moment. I want to speak to you about Shailendra.'

'Alright.' I followed him into his cabin.

He sat down on his chair. 'Please sit down.'

I took a seat, dreading his words. I, myself had already dissolved into Shailendra's eyes riddled with a million questions.

'Natasha, I want to be honest about Shailendra's condition. He has very little time. He...'

'He...what?'

Darkness loomed inside my head. Perhaps a part of me already knew the truth, but refused to acknowledge it. Though I tried, I could not control my tears. I did not know what to say.

Dr Sandeep stood up and walked over to me. He put a hand over my shoulder and said, 'You have to be brave, Natasha. I'm sure you understand. Shailendra cannot continue like this for too long. It's cruel, but as a doctor it's my duty to acquaint you with the facts.'

I wiped my eyes. It was comforting to speak to him. He returned to his chair.

'See, Natasha, his spinal cord is broken. It cannot be reconstructed no matter how hard we try. All other organs in the body are linked to it. So far, half of his body is affected. Now, slowly, all other muscles and veins are becoming dysfunctional. At the moment his brain is conscious. But in a few days—or hours—I cannot really say, he might lose that wakefulness and the ability to speak.'

'I understand, Doctor, but what can I do?'

'Yes, Natasha. What I can see...what I understand... your parents are not very well off. The professor is spending every penny on his son. Both of you need to think and consider....'

'What do I think, sir? Please tell me what to do.'

'How educated are you? What are your qualifications?'

'Sir, I've done a Master's in Psychology. I was pursuing a PhD, but was married midway through it. I could not complete my thesis or the research.'

'Not bad, Natasha. You're quite capable. How much time have you spent here in this hospital?'

'Maybe some five–six months....'

'Really? So long? You've managed everything very well—even some other patients besides Shailendra.... Yes, I remember the model who survived a suicide attempt.

You handled her very wisely. Perhaps, being a psychologist helped you erase her dilemmas. Your emotional support is very strong.'

'But sir, why isn't all my emotional support, my feelings, my love and care working in Shailendra's case? I watch my own husband die every day and there is nothing I can do about it.' Tears had welled up in my eyes again. The faded colours and suffocating smells of the hospital were overwhelming.

'There are some things in this world that are beyond the control of man, Natasha. You have to leave them to God.'

'But I don't believe in God, sir. Then why did he make my decisions for me; why does he stand between Shailendra and me?'

Dr Sandeep laughed. The room suddenly seemed to fill with light. It was a vulnerable moment for me, but he skillfully changed the subject.

'You're still very young. There is a lot to learn in life. Life is quite a complicated affair; it's not easy. It's a challenge, Natasha. Tell me, when and how did you get married to Shailendra? Don't mind, but I noticed there's a big difference between the professor and your parents. They belong to different cultures.'

'My marriage, Sir?'

'Yes, you and Shailendra.'

Dr Sandeep had surreptitiously walked into a personal

domain at a time of a painful crisis, when I had no feelings left. While the mist still lurked over me, he said, 'Natasha, I have no surgery today. I have a little time. Let me know you. I sincerely want to help you. You are standing on the edge of an explosion...or disaster. What will happen to you emotionally and financially after this? Consider me a friend and tell me about yourself. You're so young. At this age, in such a situation, is there anyone who can take care of you?'

For the first time in my life, a stranger's intervention in my personal affairs seemed like a ray of hope. I looked at his face closely. It looked grave, sensitive. He had the personality and deep values of a doctor.

'Please don't misunderstand me. I don't want anything from you personally. I've been watching you for a long time. You have looked after your husband with care and devotion. Not only that, you also care for other patients and their relatives and handle them pretty well. You have overcome the immaturity people usually have at your age.'

The ringing of his mobile phone interrupted the flow of our thoughts. He stepped out of the room to answer it. When he came back he said, 'I'm sorry, Natasha, I have to leave now. An emergency case has just come in. But I'll see you again soon. I've thought of something for your future. The next time we sit together, I'll tell you all about it, okay? And listen...there is a small get-together in the evening at... what's that place...*Simran*. I'll pick you up.'

Preoccupied with his own thoughts, he left. But he left me with my own memories of a time when *Simran* had played a great role in my life.

It was after a long time—years in fact—that I had returned to *Simran*. Uncle ji greeted me affectionately and patted my head. Sometimes words are meaningless; mere touch expresses the feelings within. Sitting at a corner table along with Dr Sandeep was a middle-aged man. From his appearance he seemed to be a doctor too, but I could not be sure.

'Come, Natasha.' Dr Sandeep stood up to introduce me. 'Meet Dr Asthana. He's the head of the department. And Asthana, this is Natasha Mehra...I told you about her. Now we have to give her a part time job and a dietician's training.'

'Dr Sandeep, you know I'm not qualified....'

'Yes, I know. That's why I'm trying. Think about your future, Natasha. You have to do something.'

I wanted to hide my eyes behind the loose end of my sari, but he said, 'No, Natasha, be brave. You know in your heart what the situation is like. You can see it every day. We are losing time.'

Dr Asthana put a hand on my shoulder. 'Look, beta, we'll do all we can to help you. You should study part time. Do a dietician's course. This nursing home has a vacancy for one. You can easily fit in. We will take care of you. You will complete it in eight or ten months. Take it up—we are with you.'

I looked at him in disbelief. There were two deep eyes behind his glasses; a gentle personality dressed in a grey suit. The age old light of humanity that was rarely visible today filled the atmosphere like a mist. It was like a backstage prompt from a friend. The same kind of friendly voice that acquainted me again now with the truth of the situation.

'As you wish. I don't really have an advisor or well-wisher in that sense.' My tearful eyes prevented words—and at this moment words would have been inadequate anyway.

I noticed an addition to the decor in *Simran* in the shape of a small aquarium. Fish of various sizes swam in the artificial sea, struck against the glass walls and retreated quietly. Sometimes they would turn their tail and their body around and go round in circles. I watched their patience with surprise. Did patience have a limit?

Dr Sandeep and Dr Asthana were still talking, but I was mesmerized by the fish tank.

Patience. How long could one maintain one's patience? How long?

'Don't these fish sleep at night?' I asked the waiter who came to collect the empty cups.

Startled he said, 'How would I know? I just switch off the lights and leave in the evening.'

'So...let's go.' Both the doctors stood up.

'What weird, nonsensical questions you ask!' The waiter glared at me. His gaze was rather rude.

'Yes, some educated people have a different kind of thought process,' Dr Asthana said, leaving a tip for the fellow. 'It could be untruth, dreaminess or something much more profound and meaningful.'

As you stepped outside the college gate, down the main road towards the left, there was a slight slope that led to a small restaurant. It was called *Simran*. It was convenient for the university crowd and the food was good. At first glance it looked like a sweets shop with hot gulab jamuns being sold on one side, while the other had a fast food counter. You could often see steaming momos being served with green chili sauce. Tea, coffee, cold drinks were easily available.

It was a contradiction of sorts. On the one hand there were hot samosas, *dalmoth*, *namakpare* served on green leaves; on the other, momos and Chinese food served on white paper plates, satiated other people's appetite. At the same time the taste of both kinds of preparation was equally authentic. Even more paradoxical was the saradarji sitting cross-legged in the middle of the restaurant upon a wooden bench, supervising everything and keeping track of the accounting.

Behind his bench, on the wall, were some lines in Gurmukhi and Hindi script:

"Sukh vele Shukrana
Dukh vele Ardas
Har vele Simran
Vahe Guru"

A huge, impactful picture of Guru Nanak was also a part of the decor.

On the second floor of that restaurant was a huge hall with tables and chairs. Our professors would sit there every evening, talking and gossiping; sometimes there were writers' forums. Some people booked the entire hall for birthday parties or other celebrations. Afternoons would see new, young women there. They were modern in their appearance, well dressed, different from college girls. Their huge sling bags and colourful stilettos were quite attractive. Students like us called the sardarji 'Uncle ji'. Once I asked him, 'Uncle ji, why do these women come here? Are they involved in some event?'

'Arrey beta, no, not a programme. It's called a kitty party. Once a month, four or five different groups gather here. They get out of their usual routine, away from their families, to enjoy themselves with friends. They gossip about this that and the other, discuss new fashions, jewellery and what not.'

He laughed. I had never seen him laugh with such abandon before.

'Uncle ji, you seem to know everything. How do you manage to find out, sitting on your bench all day long?'

'You know, beta, whenever I go upstairs to check on things, I just happen to overhear something. I like it when you call me Uncle ji. I have no daughter. Had there been one, she would probably be your age.'

'Uncle ji, what about your wife?'

'I never married.' He pointed to a woman. 'That's Devaki Behen. She is all I have. She's the one who makes wonderful gulab jamuns. Once upon a time my ancestors had sweets shops....'

Then he was silent, as though he had lost himself in a sea of memories. The past seemed to have gathered between the wrinkles on his forehead.

There was no rush at that hour. Only Mandira and I sat there having our samosas.

'Please tell us something about yourself, Uncle.' Mandira tried to enter his thoughts.

He seemed to be rummaging through old memories, trying to put pieces together. Breaking his silence he said, 'Devaki and I were very young. After Partition, it was just the two of us. We saw our parents die in front of our eyes. We stood terrified amidst the bloodshed. Satvanti Bhabhi took our hand and dragged us out of there. We came out of Rawalpindi. We were hardly five or six. We saw homes being reduced to rubble, photographs turning into ash. All alone, and stone-like herself in that situation, Bhabhi gave us support. She had tied our hands to hers with her dupatta. Sometimes, we would be on a train; sometimes on a bullock cart; sometimes in a camp. We had hardly stayed at any place for three or four days when one night we heard her screams. We were dead scared. Her dupatta fell off. I was very young, but I still remember that ghastly incident. The women in the camp became a shield around her with their sheets. After a while her screams stopped. The women put a doll in front of us. We were watching them with much surprise when Bhabhi beckoned to us to step close. "You are very young," she said, "but you must never part with this doll. Call her Simran—a mememnto of your past."

'She closed her eyes. At that age we did not know what death was. We sat with Simran in our lap. I just remember she had a large black mole just above the lips. We put her between us and went to sleep. It was quite late at night when the whole incident happened. When we woke up in the morning, there was no one around. The whole platform was empty. Simran was missing too. We had no idea where everyone had disappeared. Devaki and I howled for a long time. We shouted for Bhabhi and looked for her everywhere, but found nobody. There was deathly silence all over—the silence of a graveyard. Today when I think about it, I feel it must have indeed been one since here and there a few bodies lay burning. But yes, those people had left Satvanti Bhabhi's body buried under some stones. Fearful, my sister and I ran away. We didn't want to be separated, so we tied our hands together with a dupatta.

'Thirsty and starving we roamed the streets until we came to some kind of a shelter. It turned out to be an orphanage. A wonderful woman called Rajrani ji was in charge of the place. We stayed there for several years. We learnt to read and write. We learnt to sing bhajans and pray. I was a Sikh and remained one. Those people never asked me to cut my hair. After finishing school I left for Agra with a friend. We worked at a dhaba. I had faint memories of my father and brother running a sweets shop. It used to be pretty famous. The same ambition filled me. God was kind and here I am.'

He looked longingly at his restaurant as though an unfulfilled dream had come alive again.

'Why didn't you marry, uncle?'

'*Baliye*, I was just too busy gathering the splinters of my life. Never found the time. Didn't even think of it. I wanted to marry Devaki off, but in spite of my insistence she didn't agree. I guess both of us were simply too full of terror. How can one stay normal after going through so much? That's it. It's just the two of us for each other. I guess somewhere both of us are still looking for Simran, but how do we find her? Had she been here, she might have been like you. And then there's a mole over your lips too—just like her.'

He sighed and put two gulab jamuns on my plate. 'Go on, have them,' he said. 'You reopened some old wounds today.' He seemed absorbed in some inner turmoil.

'But it helps to talk, to share one's grief, uncle. And then I study Psychology at college. It's essential for me to know emotions well. And your experiences are so strange and different.' I was trembling within. 'Besides, I find those people very interesting who have a past. And you seem to have a hoard of memories.'

The waiter arrived.

'Sahib ji, those children have come. Should I serve them the food?'

'Yes, Chotu, please do. Why do you ask every day?'

'What children are these?' I could not help asking.

Chotu picked up the paper plates to serve the food and said, 'Sister, these are beggar children. Every day about eight or ten of them come starving and we give them food. Sahib ji wants to do it.'

'Uncle, you are great. You're doing something very noble,' said Mandira.

'Baba ji's blessings, beta,' he said. 'And then I cannot forget my own days of darkness. I have suffered starvation.' He put his hand to his chest as though suppressing his anguish.

'Uncle ji, I was already a fan of your food, now I'm also

a fan of your personality and character. Your case history will be useful to me in my studies.' I bent down to take leave. 'I will see you again soon.'

'Oh wait. You haven't finished the gulab jamuns, beta.'

'I won't be able to, uncle. Not today. But I would certainly like to know more about you.'

'Yes. Even I enjoy talking to you. You are different from the fashion-obsessed girls of today. You are the serious type, always buried in your books. Those days at our orphanage, we used to sing songs of revolution. I still remember one:

'Hum mehnatkash jawanon se ab apna hissa mangenge
ek khet nahin ek desh nahin
hum saari duniya mangenge
jab sab seedhi ho jaayegi, jab sab jhagde mit jaayenge
hum har desh ke jhande par ek laal sitara mangenge.

'Someone called Faiz wrote it I think. Whenever I sang this song with the other children in the orphanage, I would get goose bumps. I have several such incidents to relate, Natasha beta. When you talk, the old stitches tear open. The pain begins to flow again.'

'In a way it's good. You should filter these memories and agonies out of your system. Sharing such things with others leads to catharsis of the soul.'

Mandira and I carried a lot with us out of that place.

'Natasha....' My name rang in the corridor. I ran into Shailendra's room. He was screaming continuously. Despite the oxygen mask, his screams were heart-wrenching. They pierced through me. The nurse removed the mask and gave him water and slipped a pain relieving drug in the tube already inflicting his veins. Gradually, a part of Shailendra's body that was writhing with pain turned numb and heavy like the right side. As if I were under the weight of a massive rock. I felt helpless in the face of this mistiness that shrouded my mind. My own self seemed to turn into stone along with Shailendra.

'Hey, watch out,' Dr Prashant caught hold of me as I was on the verge of collapsing again. The nurse had brought him over.

'Natasha ji, you'll have to be very brave. Every day his condition...anyway, we are trying our best. Come, step outside. Shailendra won't recover consciousness for about four to six hours.'He turned to nurse Elena. 'Sister, please switch the monitor on. And change the drip.'

I went outside after the doctor. Watching Shailendra go through this ordeal was becoming more and more difficult every day. I crumpled on the bench in the corridor as though my body had given up on me. My head spun and I lost balance. Dr Prashant helped me up again.

'Come on, Natasha, let me give you some work. Sitting here all alone like this you will grow numb as a stone.

Listen—do you have any friend or relative here? I've never spotted anybody.'

'Yes, Doctor. My father's there, but he has to mind his shop and my mother has knee trouble so she can't walk much. My sister lives in Kanpur. You have already met Shailendra's father. He's a heart patient himself. It is impossible for him to watch his son in this condition. I have to look after him too. He is my only emotional support.'

I did not want to cry. I did not want to give in to depression either. Only I could keep myself afloat. I said, 'Please tell me, sir, what did you want me to do? I will do it.'

'Okay. Come with me.'

I started after him. At the other end of the corridor was a small temple where people came hoping against hope for miracles. This was their last resort. Some came when medicine could do nothing for them any more. When people lost faith in medicine, they sought alternatives to vent and address their grief: in words, chants, prayers they found catharsis. It helped to talk. Faith and atheism were no longer relevant. One simply needed an outlet for emotions. Even if it was a statue made of stone. Crossing the temple, I don't know why, I was filled with similar thoughts. I had never believed in God, never fasted or followed rules and rituals. Religion had never played a role in my life. I did not even know what it was. Only Amma used to have some pictures framed in glass on her kitchen walls. She called

God 'Thakurji'. My uneducated mother did not know any prayers or hymns. She would just light an incense stick in front of the pictures and murmur something about the welfare of her family. That was her religion. Only on Diwali I would join my parents to bow before the idols of Ganesh and Lakshmi and sing:

Jai Ganesh, Jai Ganesh, Jai Ganesh deva
Mata jaaki Parvati, Pita Mahadeva.

Just sweets, *kheele-bataashe*, diyas and incense sticks. I never even paused to think about faith. Those days...at that age, I had my own religion. Studying hard and passing the exams; nothing else. Then in college my sole aim was to become qualified enough to be able to provide a good home for my parents, away from their shanty. This ambition was synonymous with my life. Only books counted at that juncture. God with his fasts and rituals was safe in Amma's kitchen. While I was still studying, Shailendra stepped into my life unexpectedly. Marriage to him still felt like a dream. We had barely been married for two years. And now I sat lost in this hospital corridor....

'Oh, why did you stop, Natasha?' Dr Prashant's voice brought me back to the present moment.

'Sorry, sir.' I ran forward to catch up with him.

'Do you believe in God, Natasha?'

His voice had triggered my thoughts. Startled I said, 'How did you know I was thinking about God, sir?'

'I'm a doctor; I can make out what you're thinking. And it is also true that at this corner all the patients and their well wishers usually pause. Agony prompts one to believe and God gains stature.'

'Can I confess, Doctor? I do not believe in God. And after Shailendra's accident, not at all. In my middle class father's house, we never saw any priest or pandit. So I was never religious. My studies were my aspiration, my God, everything. They were my goal, my consciousness. Yet, sir, I'm not really an atheist. But you are a doctor. Do you believe in God?'

'Yes, Natasha, I do believe in God, but not in religious gurus. I find them quacks and rascals who use religion. Now even science has started recognizing God. Faith in God gives one enlightenment—great energy—which is essential when one is in the middle of an operation. You can understand, it is a meditative state. At that point nothing is mine...neither time nor the world. Only the task at hand. It's a resolve...to pull the patient out of his misery. That's all.'

'Oh, I never thought of it like that. I think your profession is a kind of surrender—complete dedication towards a patient and his suffering.'

'Yes, it is. It is a surrender to put an end to our doubts. It is a message to the self, Natasha...a message that ends the doubt that the patient cannot be relieved of his suffering.'

'You've said something really profound, Doctor. I'll have

to alter my thinking.'

'But, Natasha, you shouldn't abandon your beliefs. In fact, even your atheism is a step towards belief. In the absence of faith, man can reach the truth. Your 'questioning self'—to use a scientific term—your curiosity and the desire to seek will take you to enlightenment. And there you will find bliss, not worldliness.'

'Are you a doctor or a religious scholar?'

'Just a doctor.'

'Sir, you've been standing here for so long! Please come. An emergency case has come. A teenager's been raped. She's bleeding profusely.' Sister Dorothy's face was white.

Even a woman like her, who was usually so calm, was emotionally upset at this time. A nurse was not supposed to display emotions, but the softer side of a human being still tended to resurface from time to time. I could see multiple layers of humanity unfolding—first with Dr Prashant and now with Sister Dorothy. So was God the final culmination of life? Was he synonymous with enlightenment? Love, tenderness, misery—the hymn of life maybe?

But for me God was an undefined, mysterious entity. How was I supposed to understand Shailendra's torment? I couldn't understand why he had to endure so much.

When I returned home from the hospital, I would find Papaji sitting under the Maulsari tree, sitting pensive and frozen in one position. He had been like that all his life now.

Just then the sound of a ghazal would reach him:

Dil mein uthta hai subaho sham dhuaan,

Koi rehta hai is makaan mein abhi...

At that moment I would remember the famous psychologist, Kierkegaard: 'Sadness is my fortress. I feel quite safe hiding in it.'

I would adopt the same attitude and plonk myself beside Papaji. Startled, he would ask the same question every day, 'How is Shailendra? Any improvement? Did he manage to speak today?'

'Yes, Papaji.' There are times when words are too inadequate to express oneself.

When I returned home, Mandira was sitting on a chair in the veranda. She came running to hug me. 'Oh Natasha, what's happened!' Her tears wet my neck.

'Where were you, Mandira? I've thought of you so often. I missed you so much.'

'I went off to Paris with Zafar. I just returned this morning after two months. The moment I heard about you, I had to come.'

'Sit. I'll tell you all, but let me ask for tea first.'

'I've already brought it, beta.' Vidyawati ji put down two cups on the table.

'How are you, Vidyawati ji?'

'Arrey, what will happen to me? Only someone has cast an evil eye on the happiness of my child. What hopes we had when she was married—and look what's happened instead.'

'How did it happen? Tell me, Natasha.' She felt better after taking tea.

'I don't know how it happened, Mandira. In Singapore I was living in a dream. There was so much love and beauty. The environment filled me with a confidence I'd never had. There was nothing Shailendra did not give me.' I closed my eyes and a colourful landscape rose before me. It made me tremble.

'Oh, you're shivering.' Mandira held my hands. 'Your hands are cold as ice. Come, have some tea. Vidywati ji, please give her a shawl.'

'Alright.' Vidywati ji went inside.

'No, I'm fine, Mandira. Your emotional support overwhelmed me. I'd been waiting to share my thoughts with someone, but there was no one here. Good that you came over.'

'Yes, I'm here now. Tell me everything you've been going through.'

Vidywati ji wrapped the shawl around me. 'Arrey beta, Natasha's become a machine. Early morning she leaves for the hospital. All day she's either in Shailendra's room or sitting on the bench outside. I don't know what she eats or drinks. I send roti and sabzi with her, but sometimes she brings them back intact....For a month Shailendra was critical. I don't know how he spent a month in the ICU. Now he's in a room. He's better than before. He's also more conscious. Thank God, his brain wasn't damaged. He can talk. And even he knows that it may take a year or more for him to recover.'

'Will he recover fully? Be normal again?'

'I don't know. I cannot lie to you. Even if he recovers, God alone knows how much he will. Scientific research offers some hope, but I know miracles rarely happen.'

'You—how are you taking it? And Ved Sir?'

'Yes, dealing with Papaji is the biggest problem. Even he can see the disaster. Maybe that's why I'm retreating into a shell. Even in the numbness I can appreciate the human experience. A moment's consciousness removes me from mental dilemma and agony. If circumstances are adverse, I don't want to give in to them. Mandira, I'm trying my best to face them and rise above them.'

'Oh, that's the right attitude, Natasha. I'm proud of you.'

I don't know how long we sat there holding each other's hands.

Snapping out of old memories I said, 'Speaking of Paris, your friend, the artist...whatshisname?'

'Zafar!'

'Yes. How is he?'

'Natasha, I wanted to tell you that we're in love. I just spent two months living with him.'

'Oh, that's good news. You've found a good life partner. When are you getting married? I'm so happy for you.'

'Oh, no, no, Natasha. We're not getting married. No one will accept it—neither my parents nor Zafar himself. He doesn't want to be tied down...no commitments.'

'Then?'

'So, we'll just live together. When he can come down, he will. When I can manage to go to him, I will. I've taken a separate flat, away from my family. That's where I live. No family commitments.'

'Oh, okay. One should accept whatever life offers....'

She lay on the stretcher, groaning with pain. Even the white sheet covering her had turned crimson with blood. With every faint cry she would fold her legs. As she slipped in and out of consciousness, her mother who seemed quite a fashion-conscious woman, looked worse than her at that moment and spoke incessantly in a loud voice. 'What do I do now? Those bastards have ruined my daughter. Oh God... Such ignominy! How are we ever going to show our face in public again? Society will spit on us. Oh, what a disaster! What am I going to do?'And she began to wail.

'Please be quiet, madam, and let us attend to the patient,' said Sister Dorothy, trying to be gentle. Dheera fixed the oxygen mask to the girl's face. 'Natasha, please help her. Give her some water or she'll fall unconscious.'

I stood up and took the woman's hand and brought her to the bench where I had been sitting. Dr Sandeep had arrived. He ordered that the girl should be moved to the ICU.

'Oh Doctor, my daughter will be saved, won't she? Those monsters just mauled her! She's so young....'She began to weep again.

'Don't worry, madam. Let us attend to her. All will be well. Please be patient...Natasha, please make her sit....'

I soothed her trembling body and handed her a glass of water. 'Please have it and try to calm down. Crying and wailing will not help the situation. Please relax.' I took her hands in mine. I wanted to help, but she jerked them away and said, 'How can I calm down? My daughter's just been through a mass rape! She's suffered such great injustice. Those guys haven't left her with an iota of dignity. How will she ever face society again? How will she live with the stigma? And what about us...the family?'

'I admit what happened was wrong at every level. But please have courage. You will need to show a great deal of grit. She's still a child...very young, but you're the mother. Only you can help her out of this state of shock. If you lose hope and patience yourself, how will you be of any use to her?

'Yes, you're right. My mind isn't working. Such a catastrophe; it's shaken our world. That too, a few stupid schoolteachers...I won't spare them.' She hid her face in her dupatta and wept. I made some coffee and brought it to her. After a while an office peon brought some hospital documents in a folder. 'Madam, you need to fill these forms. Will you come to the office or sit here...?'

She sat down on the bench. 'No, I'm fine here. There's a lot of rush at the counter. And many of them recognize me. I will complete all the formalities sitting here.'

'Okay. You will need to arrange for funds too.'

'Alright.' She finished her coffee and sat pensively for a bit. Then she looked at me and said, 'I wanted to speak to my husband, but in this confusion I misplaced my phone....'

'Never mind. You can use mine.' I opened my purse and handed my mobile to her.

'Oh thanks.' She dialled the number and began to talk. 'Rajesh, I've brought Priya to the hospital. How long will you take to come? What? What did you say? I shouldn't use her real name? Not even the surname? Why...? Oh, I see. It'll give us a bad name, no? It could be the headline in tomorrow's papers. But what will you tell the others? Say anything—she's been sent abroad for studies or something. Maybe that'll be the best... So you won't come? Someone will come down from the office with the cash? Okay....'

Suddenly she noticed me sitting nearby. 'Oh, you heard the conversation. May I ask who you are?'

'I...I am a patient's relative like you. My husband's admitted in this hospital, in that room nearby. I sit here every day on this bench.'

'Oh, thanks.' She handed my phone back to me.

'But you must at least report this to the police. It's imperative for the rapists to be charged with the crime. How will you punish them otherwise? And those savages who did this to the poor child and ruined her life. Rape is a worse crime than murder.'

'Please leave her to me. I also have to think about the family's esteem. You know, we're a well-known family in Agra. It's a huge empire. My husband owns....'

She stopped and began to fill up the form. Only I knew that the raped girl's real name was Priya, nobody else. But she filled in Pooja instead and signed her own name as Shalini Gupta. Even though Dr Sandeep tried to reason with her, she did not give in but maintained silence instead. The ghastly incident was never reported to the police.

Then she left Pooja to herself and disappeared stealthily. Consequently, her daughter, left alone in her gloomy room, sank into depression.

Two days later she was shifted into a room close to Shailendra's. I used to watch all the happenings closely from the bench. Her mother, Shalini Gupta, used to come late in the evening to visit her, hiding herself from the crowd. But she had arranged for a maid to sit there all day with Pooja. The maid only sat around.

Pooja's mental health deteriorated every day. I watched her slip further into deep depression every day. She would scream if she was touched and was too terrified to open her eyes. Often she would have nightmares and start trembling. At mealtimes I would go to her, try to talk to her and manage to feed her a little...or do whatever I could.

Dr Prashant handed Pooja's case to Harry. Thanks to his efforts she improved a little. But her eyes were always glued to the door. She waited for her parents to show up, but they never did. Her father did not appear even once.

Pooja spoke only to Harry. He was the one who took her outside in the garden on a wheelchair. Sometimes he would play cards with her; at other times they would play carom. At those times they would laugh openly. I found this camaraderie between them fascinating. But the mystery of Pooja's parents' lives was beyond me.

Papaji had come in. His face looked pale, as though sinking under some invisible weight. His body had bent weathering the various storms in his life. Sometimes I felt that even the human body could alter enough to resemble ancient ruins.

So was I really standing between two such ancient ruins? And why?

I slipped my hand out of Shailendra's in a hurry and stood up. Papaji stepped closer to him and asked in a heavy voice, 'How are you, beta?' His voice was tearful. His hand, resting on Shailendra's shoulder, was trembling.

'Please sit down, Papaji.' I distracted him from his questions. 'Come, we'll have some coffee. I'll just get it. I will have some too. I had been waiting for it for a while.'

'Yes, bring some. Let me sit here.'

'Don't you have to go to the university, Papaji?'

'Natasha, it's 26th January today; did you forget?'

'Oh, yes.'

At the open portion of the window some pigeons fluttered and settled themselves. Along with them were a few brown coloured birds. Shailedra stared at them for quite some time.

'Shailendra, should I get you some coffee?'

'No...no, Natasha. Listen...these pigeons reminded me—in Ajmer there used to be pigeon fighting. All the friends used to get together in a dilapidated building in an ancient mohalla. It was called Haji Manzil. We had heard some rich man had started it. It's been going on since then.'

'What was that?' I wanted him to keep talking, to keep his memories alive. It was essential for his brain, for its power of recall.

'Yes, Natasha. We would go to the fifth floor of their mansion. Chishtiji, the owner of the birds would already be there on the terrace, standing proudly in his sherwani. He would call out to his pigeons in a special tone—"Brr brr" or "ghrr ghrr..." which was probably the way his birds spoke. Soon the whole sky would be full of colourful birds chirping away. It was an amazing scene. Then Chishti mian would invite them closer and the birds would follow him obediently.

'At that time Chishti mian was also attached to the mosque. He was famous and respected. He always introduced us very proudly to the gathering of his 500 birds that he had got from various countries. Some had come especially from Basra in Iraq, some from Iran. And the more astonishing part was that he had given all of them names. He called one 'Chirage Roshan' and another 'Chashme Bulbul'. And when he called, the bird would raise its beak and hop over to his palm.

'You will be surprised to know, Natasha, that he treated them like royalty.'

'How so?' I was amazed.

'He would give them ghee, almonds, raisins, etc. to eat which birds don't usually get.'

'But birds eat chillies or raw fruit. I used to watch Amma scatter millet at the street crossing. A lot of birds would gather there.'

'Maybe he gave them that too, but the royal food was

a special treat and he would talk about it with great pride.'

'This game must have been a pretty expensive affair.'

'Yes, of course. But betting did not involve any money those days. The winner would take ten pigeons from the loser as recompense.'

'There was no cinema or television then when they started the game. These were the only means of entertainment.'

'I'm talking about my university days, not olden times. Some families continue the ancestral hobbies even today. It's not so grand now, but it's there. My friends who live there told me that now this passion has indeed become very expensive because the maintenance of the birds is expensive. In a few years it will be history. Only the stories will remain. Like the old ruins.'

'Oh.' I don't know why I felt a tinge of sadness.

Before I could slip into depression, Papaji took charge of the situation.

'Shailendra, it's an entertaining game. Good to hear about it. And then it's the 26th today.' Then he turned to me, 'Get some coffee, Natasha. Then you've to leave for your course.'

'What course?'

'Natasha has joined a dietician's course here.'

Shailendra's eyes reflected a dilemma.

'I'll get the coffee.'

'Yes....'

When there are no words, no sympathy, and even hope

disappears, then that empty space needs to be filled by something or the other.

As I stepped out, Sister Dorothy ran into me. Taking my hand she said, 'You know, Natasha, that rape case...the victim's mother has given neither her real name nor her real surname. They have not even informed the police till now. The girl belongs to some well-known family. The father has not been to see his daughter even once, fearing people will recognize him. Can you imagine to what extent humans can be cruel and selfish. And that poor girl is going into depression. She's stopped speaking. She's wilting within.'

'Yes, the wounds are very deep. It was a mass rape. And those men injured her so badly.'

'Alright...let me see where Harry is. He is the one looking after her. I find Pooja's mother a fool. She's more bothered about the world than her daughter. And, Natasha, I wanted to tell you we have a festival on Friday. You must come. We all pray together. It's Easter. Harry especially wants to pray for you and Pooja.'

She turned and left. But walking slowly I reached the corner of the hospital where the temple stood. Some people had etched a Radha–Krishna statue into its wall. The carving looked beautiful and lifelike as though the flute in Lord Krishna's hands would begin to play any moment.

The image some renowned artist had carved into the wall was a combination of different religions. Besides their major symbols and couplets, he had calligraphed lines in Urdu and Gurmukhi, including parts of the *Guru Granth Sahib*. In one corner he had drawn the crucifixion of Christ. Even Buddha and Mahavira were there on the same wall and in the same picture. Dr Prashant had told me that the artist had received a special award for this unique picture.

And I did not believe in God. I had never bowed in front of Amma'sThakurji in her little kitchen. But whenever I came and stood near this carving, it did fill me with a strange energy. I don't know if it was a fantasy or real. I did not know God at all. Then? Somehow I had begun to feel the flute was playing or that someone was reciting the couplets in a soft voice. They were chants beyond my comprehension since they were in Punjabi, but their sweet hum filled me with warmth. Just walking past that temple, all my negative thoughts were replaced by positivity and hope.

Whenever my worries about Shailendra grew, I would come and stand near this picture. Often Harry would come, bow before it and hum a prayer.

'Oh, this boy just doesn't listen!' Zubaida from room no 18 was trying to drag the young man with all her might. There was no softness in the voice. Had the entire world turned rude and bitter?

'Get up, you rascal.' Zubaida wiped the sweat off her forehead as though trying to wipe an old statement off a blackboard.

The young man dropped her hand and clutched mine instead. 'Spare me, Ammi. I'll be grateful if you can stop her, sister. I just want to sit out there in fresh air.'

His speech gave the impression he was a gentleman. His face too seemed bright.

'Please...do let him sit....'I made a feeble attempt to intervene.

'No, madam, this boy is crazy. If something untoward happens, no amount of explanation will help.'

'Ammi, please!' He opened the windows and began to breathe in the cool air. His desires seemed to soar along with a flock of birds in the sky. Some inner conflict made his hands tremble. He still held my fingers tightly.

His mother stepped closer again. 'Come, beta, let's go home. It's getting late. We have to travel far.'

'I don't want to travel far! Rukhsana won't be able to live. Those heartless bastards won't spare her. And I...I won't be able to live without her.'

'Come on, Sahil. Get up, child. Let's get home and talk.' His mother tried to avoid meeting my eyes.

'Go, go with your mother.' I tried unsuccessfully to free my hand from his grasp.

'No, no, Ammi will lock me up in this room again. This

is not our home. And I...I am sick of the darkness.'

In his nervousness he closed his eyes. As though despite his mother's presence, some deep sense of insecurity clouded around him. He wanted to get away.

Robbing someone of their freedom is also an act of violence. No mother can do it. But did I really need to know the truth of their situation? The scene froze in that moment. All three of us fell silent, trying to contextualize our individual pain.

Then all of a sudden, the boy stood up gathering his wits. He looked like an uprooted tree, lying cut off from its roots, as if life itself had ostracized him.

Sister Roma arrived right at that time and tried to take him away. 'Come on, Sahil, let's go.'

He began to mumble incoherently, 'Where? Rukhsana is waiting for me there, isn't she?'

'Yes, come.' The nurse played her role.

After they had left, the mother took my hand and led me to her room. We sat down quietly on the chairs. The television was on. There was some programme on puppets running at that time. The characters changed in every scene. Sometimes they staged the rule of Lord Rama, sometimes Sita's kidnapping, sometimes the killing of Ravana. And then the other avatars would take over just as easily. The scenes changed quickly enough outside. But it was so difficult to change them within one's mind and heart. Operated through strings, the puppets, unburdened by emotions could still manage to convey myriad scenes through their leaping and dancing, entertaining the audience, while the puppeteer cleverly managed to engage them. But the strings entangling the soul were operated very differently. The inner truths could not be revealed in the confusion of the universe. They lay scattered. Puppets were tied to weak threads, but the threads of life were far stronger.

'Forgive me, beta,' Zubaida broke the silence. 'My son has lost his mind due to the tragedy. His wife was seven months pregnant. He tried to save her from the rioters, but they got to her. They spared him, but who spares women? During the attack they assaulted her, and once they were done, ripped her stomach. The baby died. Rukhsana, too, died. Who can forget that terrible incident? Had it been anybody else, he would have lost his mind too.' She began to weep. Somewhere in the background I could hear a voice saying, 'I have to save Rukhsana!'

The strings of the puppets had broken. Slowly, the control of the puppeteers was fading. Rama–Ravana, princes and princesses, Salim and Anarkali...all were packed away together in the same box. Rukhsana, Sahil, Shailendra... playing with life, the tangled strings, the ups and downs, the brokenness....

I had just stepped out of Zubaida's room and sat down on my bench when suddenly the Sardar uncle and Devaki ji from *Simran* appeared beside me.

'Oh, it's you, uncle...how come you're here...? You shouldn't have troubled yourself.'

'It's you who've been dealing with all the trouble, beta. When we heard about Shailendra, we couldn't stop ourselves. We thought we'd come and see him. How is he now, *baliye*?'

Some questions have no answers. My silence, and the smell of medicines in the corridor was synonymous with their query—and the circumstances.

Devaki ji opened a cardboard box and pushed it towards me. 'Take, beta. I brought you some samosas I made myself. Have some.'

'Eat, beta.' Sardar uncle put his hand on my shoulder. 'You are very fond of them, aren't you? You look so lifeless. And you used to be so lively...like a locust. You could never sit still.'

Their love and affection in that moment established a bond between us. I could hardly say anything. I sat down on the bench quietly. The samosas in the box rekindled a forgotten desire for food. My aching heart accepted the hunger and I began to eat. Their eyes too filled up with tears at the sight of mine.

Two boys brought in Sahil on a stretcher. Zubaida ji accompanied them. He was groaning despite his unconscious state.

I leapt to my feet. 'What happened, aunty? Why did Sahil faint?'

'Beta, he's been given an electric shock. What to do? We had no option. Don't know when we'll be free of religious conflicts, hatred, the increasing distance between people....'

When I told Sardar uncle about the accident, he lost himself in the past. From the corner of the cursed darkness he emerged and said, 'Beta, I remember—when we were at the camp, we were very young. We did not understand religion. When people said, "We are Hindus; they are Muslim," I would stare hard at their faces, but I could find no difference. All of us had similar features.'

Devaki aunty had covered her head with her dupatta. 'But Bhai ji, do you remember they wore round caps on their head?'

'Yes. Even on the train they were chopping off heads that did not have round topis on them. Or they would force some boys to pull their pyjama strings and peep inside.' He looked at the ground. 'But we knew nothing. Someone at the refugee camp told us we were sardars—Devaki and I. That is when I wore the *pagdi*.' Once again Simran found a mention in the ancient ruins of memory. 'Our only regret is that we did not find Simran. God knows whether she ended up as a Hindu or a Muslim. God knows where the last souvenir of our home disappeared.'

'But uncle, you made her immortal. She is there in

Simran, very much with you, a part of your generosity.'

'Perhaps...alright, beta, we must leave now.' Devaki aunty's plastic foot limped under the base of her salwar, but she had an imposing personality. So...isn't every life a silent narrative of some cruel accident? Sahil's cries floated through closed doors and scattered in the air outside, communicating some inhuman anomalies.

Sister Dorothy said, 'Natasha, tomorrow we'll be on leave. It's Easter tomorrow.'

'Oh yes. But why is Easter celebrated, sister? I have no idea.'

'You know, Natasha, on Easter, Jesus Christ walked out of his grave. He gave up the attachment to his body—the attachment we all have.'

'Sorry, sister. I never learnt about Christianity or Christians.'

'Natasha, Christ was not a human; he was the son of God. All his life he was humiliated by humans. He had been hurt a lot, so much so that the sweat on his forehead wasn't just sweat but drops of blood.' She closed her eyes. 'He was injured by human emotions—by the wounds given to him by some commoner.' By now Sister Elena had joined us.

'Yes, Natasha, he suffered a great deal. His life and times

were full of trials and tribulations. And, you know, the day he was to be crucified, he had to tow the cross himself—carry it on his own shoulders.'

Sister Dorothy was shaking. I put my arms around her. It felt as though she could experience the pain of Christ herself.

'Sister, you're usually so brave. You give me courage all the time. You have looked after Shailendra all this while and thanks to you he's better...but today?'

Sister Elena intervened. 'Sister Dorothy is a true Christian. She follows her religion very seriously. We learn a lot from her. She is our head, Natasha.'

'Do you know, Natasha, Christ delivered his most crucial sermon just before his death; that speech is the gist of Christianity. The crucifixion, the entire process was a display of the pinnacle of life. In his crucifixion he achieved immortality. But did he really not die, Natasha? There is certainly some percentage of difference between God and matter.'

'So can matter...a dead body...be God, sister?'

By this time we had arrived at a painting on the hospital wall—the scene of crucifixion where Christ lay helpless. I began to think about what my poor Shailendra had done, so that he was being punished with the same kind of agony.

'You know, Natasha, this is a day of awakening for us—to understand something as unrelenting as death, to come to terms with the truth of our existence.'

'And that we should learn to overcome our physical and mental weaknesses. We should try and rebuild our confidence and self esteem. Believing in our 'being', in our existence, brings about a balance in our lives, Natasha. Self confidence is crucial when one becomes aware of it.'

I was staggered. What a brilliant thought. Was this a hospital? Were these nurses—or some religious leaders?

'Natasha, do you know what message Easter conveys? It teaches us to step out of our worldliness and move towards an unknown, invaluable and beautiful future.'

'Oh sister, you've brought me to a strange truth. How did you learn so much?'

'During my nursing days I read the complete Christian mythology, Natasha.' Sister Dorothy's eyes shone bright.

'Anyway, sister, I have enjoyed talking to you. Because in the stillness of my mind, when I hear the footsteps of death, it makes me tremble. My feelings, dreams, emotions are folding up into nothingness. What do I do?'

'Dear Natasha, take care of yourself, of your being. You have a spark as Dr Sandeep says. You have inner light. We have been observing how you have balanced your life during the last six months. You spend the entire day on that bench sometimes. Along with caring for your husband, you read fat books. Harry told us you help Pooja as well. You are really sweet.'

Sister Dorothy kissed my hand.

'Thank you, sister. You too give me so much love. Will Harry be absent too?'

'Yes, he will be on leave too.'

'Okay. Then I will take care of Pooja.'

'And you must come to our cottage on Easter day. Or whenever you have the time.'

'Your cottage!'

'Yes, behind the hospital, as you cross the garden. Yes, right there.' She pointed to a building behind the hospital.

Sitting by myself in the afternoon I wondered if I should go and visit Sister Dorothy or Harry in their cottage and see the church too. Shailendra was asleep after taking his injection. I had to go there on Easter anyway, so I found out the way to the staff quarters and made my way behind the hospital. There was a narrow path flanked by gardens on either side. Here and there you could see Neem and Peepal trees and some trees laden with red flowers. The walls were covered with bright pink bougainvilleas. Multiple rows of trees and assorted plants defined the expanse. Some white flowers also stood out with their plastic beauty, looking awkward. God knows which part of the year they had been planted and by whom? But all the plants were lost in themselves, offering shelter and spreading fragrance; some had shed their flowers.

Despite that, the flowers, the lush green leaves and grass hummed their own tune that soothed the mind. The hospital was quite old. Perhaps the garden was equally old. Maybe thirty or forty years or more. But time had not allowed the garden to languish—even though Agra constantly faced water shortage. I was pleased that there was at least something that stood solid in the face of adversities. In spite of the changing times and the cultural gap it maintained its old features. I liked the colourful atmosphere and the greenery. A little further there was a row of conjoined rooms. They had a long, common veranda. I went and stood before the first room. On the wall near the door, a blue nameplate showed Harry's name. The door was shut. When I knocked, Harry opened the door and welcomed me with a smile.

'He said in a loud voice, 'Arrey, Natasha didi, you here! Come in, come in. What a pleasant surprise.'

'Thanks, Harry. I just came to see you. Sister Dorothy invited me a couple of times. I thought I'd familiarize myself with the route before Easter. This is the time for your rest. I hope I didn't disturb you.'

'No, no...in fact, I'm very happy you came, didi. Please take a seat.' He pointed to a chair. I noticed the room was neat and clean. An iron cot stood against the wall covered by a sheet with blue checks on it. A small table stood against another wall; it had a pile of books on it. A portrait of Christ hung on the wall with his bright, impactful eyes. A stream of light emerged from a source near his heart. Next to it an incense stick burnt on a wooden platform spreading a sweet scent and faith in the air. A half burnt candle too lay upon a small plate.

'Come didi, come and see my certificate.' He took my hand and made me get up. 'See, this is my nursing certificate.' It lifted him above his physical weaknesses and mental difficulties and gave him a wide canvas. Breaking my string of thoughts he said, 'You know, didi, when I was born I was ill. The doctors said it was 'Down's Syndrome.'

'Yes. But you are brave and you have this certificate. You've studied up to class ten, Harry. You can speak both English and Hindi. Your parents?'

'I know nothing about them, Natasha didi. I don't even know what my original religion is. The Christian Association has an orphanage called 'Hope'. It is run by the priests and nuns. I grew up there. The Padre Sa'ab we called Father named me Harry Masih. That became my identity.' His voice broke and his body trembled a little. I held his hand to steady him. 'Due to my illness, my parents left me by the roadside. Father, the head of the church, found me at the garbage dump and brought me up. He never let me feel I was different from other 'normal' children—a victim of Down's Syndrome. His quivering voice was strangely sweet and reflected self confidence.

'I had the blessings of Christ that I managed to achieve

this much. Father enrolled me into the nursing course so I could stand on my own feet. Otherwise, I would have been begging at the corner of some street, alone and uncared for.

He began to cry. I put my hand on his shoulder lovingly. 'Come on, you are so very brave. You are helping others in need with such assurance. Their blessings count, Harry. I'm sure your sincerity and service is much appreciated at the hospital. And I can see how much effort you put into looking after Pooja, trying to restore her spirits, like an elder brother. If she recovers, it will be because of your hard work—your love and dedication.

'Yes, these are like exams I need to pass, Natasha ma'am.' There was a question mark in his eyes.

'Call me didi, Harry. I have no brother. I like it when you call me didi.' I stepped forward and grasped both his hands. 'Tell me how you came to this hospital.'

'Sister Dorothy gave me this job. Father had told her about me. She is a very nice woman. She supports everybody—all the nurses and other staff. Dheera, Miss Mohini, Miss Eliza—she brought them all here. We are a family here. We eat together at the same table at the mess. We celebrate our festivals together. Most of us are orphans, discarded and dumped by our parents.'

I came out of Harry's room and went ahead. There were no nameplates on a couple of doors, but they had something or the other hanging on them. A simple lace made of pearls or coloured festoons that made the place alive.

One of the rooms had Sister Dorothy's name on it. The door was half open. That is why I walked in without hesitation. It was a large room; the window was open. Sunlight filtered in through the mesh and lit it up. The bed was made and a few clothes hung on pegs, but what I saw shook me. Sister Dorothy stood leaning against a wall. Her body was bare. Miss Eliza's lips rested against her big, dark nipples. Sister Dorothy's eyes were closed, but her fingers were busy under Eliza's skirt. Strange sounds. Strange smells. I stood flabbergasted. It was amazing that they were so immersed in themselves that they were completely oblivious to my presence and never heard me come in. I dropped the curtain hastily, turned and ran. I did not even have the courage to say sorry for my brazenness. I don't know why I dared to transgress. But some crimes are committed inadvertently. Sweating nervously I returned to the corridor in the hospital.

I did not even have the courage to go up to the carved picture near the temple that usually gave me solace.

When I returned home I found Papaji reading on the sofa in his room. Seeing me Vidyawati ji said, 'You must be tired, beta. Should I lay the table?'

'Please wait. Let me have a bath first. I'll just take ten minutes.' I don't know why I felt embarrassed looking them in the eye. Was it the scene I had witnessed in Sister Dorothy's room? I still had not recovered from it. I thought a bath might help me shake it off my mind.

'Natasha beta, what are you studying these days? Bhaisahab mentioned you're doing some course.'

'Yes, Vidyawati ji. Dr Sandeep has got me enrolled into a dietician's course. During the day I stay with Shailendra. In the evening I go for my classes.'

'What is that, beta? Something to do with Medicine?'

'No Vidya behen, this course helps you understand the problems related to your diet. It tells you what sick people or obese people should eat and what they should avoid. Obesity is also a kind of disease,' Papaji tried to explain.

'But how can this problem exist in a country where people don't even have enough to eat? Even hunger is a disease. Only people who have too much can suffer from something like obesity. Right, Natasha?'

'Gandhi ji suggested discipline for such people too. It was called fasting. He encouraged this practice so that more food could be saved. Even in the ancient times the sages, considering God as the giver of food, adopted fasting as an integral part of religious rituals. They thought it would ensure the hungry would receive enough food,' Papaji replied. His explanation was an eye-opener for me too.

'And Vidywati ji,' I added, 'The wrong kind of food we enjoy so much during our student days—pizzas, burgers, potato chips, etc. are actually more dangerous than cigarettes. This course acquaints me with what's healthy and unhealthy, what's nutritious, what the patients should eat so that they can digest it even if they spend most of their time lying flat on the bed.'

'Oh, one needs to think of so many things? I just know when hunger pangs strike, one can digest anything. In our time most of the food used to be healthy and hygienic. My mother used to cook early morning after a bath, on a fire built from wood and dung cakes. She did not even wear stitched blouses those days, just a clean dhoti. Food was also clean, homemade and very tasty. She would not allow us in the kitchen unless we had bathed.'

'How strange! She did everything on her own? My mother kept Urvashi and me engaged in the kitchen all the time. But yes, she fasts. And in our neighbourhood some aunties used to fast during Ramzan. They just went on for so long! They did not even have water during those fasts.'

'Yes. You must fast on Karva Chauth for Shailendra to live long—okay, Natasha?'

'Sure. Last year I was in Singapore, so I didn't realize

when it came. This year I will certainly do it.'

Papaji wiped his eyes, trying to hide it from me. I was careful with mine. I steered the conversation away from the subject.

'Thanks, Papaji. Vidyaji, I will include this religious form of fasting in my course. The ways of the world are strange that tie hunger to God.'

'Yes, Natasha. Fasting was a way of worship for Gandhi ji. That is why his Satyagraha set such a strong example before us.'

When I reached there, the Easter celebrations were on. In the hall, straight in front, there was a long, high table. At its centre stood a picture of Christ. The flowers in front added to the beauty. Candles burnt on either side of the picture. The scent of incense pervaded the atmosphere. The padre, dressed in a long black gown, sat on a chair. The choir was about to finish singing the hymns. The sermon had perhaps ended already. All the people were seated. Padre Sa'ab stood up and sprinkled water upon the bowed heads before him. Everybody stood up and began to embrace each other. Sister Dheera held me by the hand and took me forward. 'Welcome, Natasha. Good you decided to come. Come and take Padre Sahab's blessings.'

'Yes.' I followed her quietly. The whole experience was

new to me, as the constantly changing colours of life.

Everybody was taking turns to bend to receive blessings from the padre. They would touch his robe to their forehead. All the faces were ordinary—like mine—yet extraordinary. I observed the entire process closely. All of us, in the grip of our fears and worry for our loved ones, seemed to be seeking some kind of a sanctuary here. Perhaps most were looking for help and reassurance at a time of anxiety and self-doubt. And the other question that shook me was—how had so many people really converted? Dheera dragged me on. 'Come, Natasha. Take his blessings for the sake of Shailendra's health.'

'Oh yes.' I stepped closer to him. I put my palms together and wished him and touched his robe to my forehead.

'God bless you, my child.' He put his hand on my head. A gentle personality; his hands were wrinkled with age.

'Sir, thanks.'

'Her husband is in great pain, Father. He has had a major accident.'

'Oh, I am sorry.' He sprinkled the holy water over me. 'He will be all right. Jesus will help.'

'Father, if you will not take it otherwise, may I ask you a question? I am a psychologist. I wish to understand the psychology behind religious conversion...If you find my question offensive, please forgive me.' I brought my palms together once again.

'No, my child. I can answer your question. You must know. Why just me, most people here were born in families where the only religion was hunger. It was a question of survival. People needed to earn to assuage their hunger and live.'

'But, sir, there were other religions too.'

'Yes, there were. Even I wondered about it. I tried to analyze the reasons according to my own education. I realized that religion and faith are not hereditary. They are not something bequeathed by the family. It's a discovery. Religion is an experiment, a research. We need to find the road. It's a road of discovery. Once we find it, it becomes the leading route; a road of inner transformation.'

'Look at us today, Natasha,' said Dheera. 'Most of us were born in Dalit or Mehtar communities. It was our job to clean the garbage or sweep the floors. People wouldn't touch us with a bargepole. We were considered untouchables.'

'Your God is omniscient, all-knowing. Then why did he create such discrimination amongst his people?' Father gave me a questioning glance.

Rosy had tears in her eyes. 'You don't know, Natasha, my dadi has never worn any shoes or slippers. In winter or summer she used to be busy on the road with a broom, barefoot. Her scarred feet sometimes bled. She would rub oil on them or tie them with a cloth and go to bed.

Dheera removed her pretty shoes.

'But your culture! You must have been taught something of Hindutva in childhood. What did you do with that ?'

'What culture? We weren't given any, Natasha. Forget about culture, our ancestors were never even allowed to go to school or enter a temple.'

'If you belong to a certain religion, it inspires you. You can follow its dictates. In our case it's simply love and compassion that inspires us. The missionaries picked us up from the road and embraced us. They made us sit on chairs, gave us lives that we could never have imagined though every living being has a right to it. Your religion did not give us all that. Now all of us are educated. Today we understand culture, we understand Hindutva, but it is...or was...like a prison to us. Walls are not made of bricks and mortar, but fanaticism and superstition, madam. We broke out of those prisons. Christianity was one route...or religion...whatever you wish to call it. It's up to you to choose. You have to look for the truth within and think where you wish to reach. What is your goal? Love or ostracism?'

Father's hand resting on my head trembled a little. I don't know how many bitter experiences, painful experiences and insults were reflected in it.

'Okay, let's go, Father. It's time to cut the cake. You are getting late.' Sister Dorothy invited everybody for tea. Harry took my hand and said, 'Come, Natasha.' And he brought me outside.

I had so much to unlearn. I was annoyed at my own naivety and intellectual emptiness. The people here had risen above their surroundings. They knew all about self-love, wishes and wants, while I still struggled with myself to understand which direction I was supposed to take, where I was supposed to go. Me. Only me. Not the others.

That morning when I reached Shalendra's room, the mask was off. He was sitting propped up against the pillows, perhaps waiting for me.

'How are you, Shailendra?' I asked. 'Look, I've brought some kheer for you. Would you like to have some now or later...?'

'Later, Natasha. Come, sit with me. The pain is a little better right now.' His eyes were moist and heavy.

'See, didn't I say you would recover soon? Dr Sandeep, Dr Raizada and Dr Prashant have been trying their utmost...Yes, of course it will take some time. Just a little patience. Be patient.'

'I'm amazed at your patience, Natasha. I've seen you suffer so much. Night and day you're in the hospital. What do you eat and drink? How is the house being managed? Papaji? Just two years of married life—and what did you get!'

'To be honest, Shailendra, it's some deep bond—some

strong cord that has kept me tied to you. When I had just met you, a wave of love rose in my heart. That love pervaded my being. I dedicated myself to you, body and soul. What haven't you given me—a fulfilling life, travels abroad, a dream-like life in Singapore that broadened my horizons and polished not just my appearance but my entire personality.' I closed my eyes. I wanted to relive that dream within. Was it a dream or did it really happen? But the tragedy—the car that butchered Shailendra...it shattered everything. My body began to tremble at the memory.

'I want to live, Natasha. I want to love you with my heart and soul. The love that you speak of—is it really so strong, so powerful that it can transform someone and change his entire personality?'

'Yes, Shailendra. You must have heard the Hindi axiom '*dhai akhshar prem ka padhe so pandit hoye,*' that is, he who understands love gains wisdom. If you're in love, you don't need temples or mosques. The love you feel awakens the God within you. Shailendra, love is an individual religion. Existential. Other emotions don't count.'

'Oh Natasha, your words are so interesting. That's why I want to live—for you, for me, for Papaji...I want to give him the home he never had. But my body doesn't cooperate.'

'Don't worry, Shailendra. You're being treated in the best possible way. You will be alright.'

'Where we stand today, you and I, is the point where

the sun rises. Yes, Natasha, this is where the sunrise will happen and I will stand up on my own feet. And I will be able to love you to my heart's content.' He pulled my hands with his with whatever strength he had. The sea of pain he felt reflected in his eyes. Sympathy was fast dissolving into utter silence, because sometimes words themselves become meaningless.

Suddenly Shailendra said, 'What have you become? You have neither good clothes nor any lipstick. How pale your face looks. And no bangles on your wrists? Please, Natasha, don't punish yourself for my agony.'

'I left the house in a hurry, that's all. Vidyawati ji hasn't been keeping well. Papaji too had to leave early. I was getting late, so just left as I was. Tomorrow, I'll dress up properly, okay?'

I was trying my best to maintain my composure. Outside the window a slight drizzle had started, an unseasonal shower. A little bird sat quietly amongst a flock of pigeons.

'Listen, Natasha...the first time I saw you, this is how you were...less of a student and more of a hermit...with a pile of books in your hands...but I wanted to make you into a regal figure—the kind of women I had seen in Ajmer where a friend from a royal family lived.' Suddenly, he began to pant. I gave him some water.

'Shailendra, please don't talk anymore. Your health is failing. Where's the oxygen mask? Let me call the nurse....'

'No, Natasha. Let me talk before I have no breath left.'

I locked his trembling fingers with mine. This was the healthy hand. The other had gone numb. It could feel no touch and it lay limply on the bed.

'Listen, Natasha...I like your beautiful wheatish skin though my mother was rather fair. I saw her at a fashion show on television once.'

'You're remembering your mom? Should I try and get in touch with her?'

'Oh no, no...her rejection haunts both Papaji and me, Natasha. Don't. I was saying...you should never use that Fair & Lovely cream they show on television....' His breath came quick.

I wrapped him in my arms and said, 'Don't say anything, Shailendra. Let me speak. Even touch has a language; it conveys emotions. I will understand whatever you wish to say.'

'Yes. That will be great.'

'Let me tell you something. Before I met you, I had never loved a man. I had no idea what love was...what kind of emotion. I simply wanted to study. I hadn't thought about my life or made any future plans. That's when you appeared out of the blue. Forget about love, there wasn't even any friendship between us. We just decided to marry. Isn't that strange?'

He tried to laugh. 'I took a fancy to you.' He put my hand over his heart.

'But Shailendra, you were so handsome, so well read, so well educated—I couldn't believe it when you said, "Natasha, just come into our lives."'

We stood at that point in our past...stood there for quite a while.

Shailendra said, 'I did the right thing. And then Papaji praised you so much from time to time.'

'You know, Shailendra...there is a study in Psychology called Synthesis that implies joining or being joined together. Psychologists say religion has the same process—from atom to monolith. To join together until nothing remains separate. I was writing a paper on Synthesis when you walked into my life. At that time the picture on the wall had a sun in its landscape. I don't know how that sunlight pervaded your body in such a way that that those rays emerged from it and warmed the cockles of my heart. God knows how it happened. Strange radioactivity. Do you think it's easy to hold sunrays in your hands? If that is called love, then I began to love you, Shailendra.'

I had put my lips to his eyelids. The forehead was warm like the sun; the veins throbbed. With my moist lips I wanted to soak all his anguish, all his pain.

'Shailendra, I could not believe my luck. Nor could my parents. Amma used to say Lord Krishna had played his flute. I felt my rocking, directionless boat had at last found an anchor.'

'But why did the river's love, the river's bank change into a tsunami, Natasha? What happened? He touched his limp hand with his other one weakly. 'Why did the storm have to wreak havoc in our lives?'

'Storms end, Shailendra. Tsunamis die down. They must—for your sake and mine; for Papaji's sake. You must live, Shailendra.'

'Come, let's wait for that day too.' His voice reflected the weakness of his body. 'I don't know how Papaji is taking this disaster.' The pain flowed through his veins. 'He spent so many years living, providing for me. He devoted everything to make a better future for me...and I....'

'Shailendra, we haven't given up hope. You're getting better; you'll be fine. Then you can look after Papaji all you want.'

'Natasha, have you ever read Papaji's diary? Try and read it stealthily; he shouldn't come to know, okay?'

'Oh really? Papaji writes a diary? I didn't know.'

The door opened and Papaji entered. We exchanged a meaningful look.

'How are you, beta?' asked Papaji.

I stood up. 'Come, Papaji, please sit down. Don't you think Shailendra is better than before? Please talk to him. I'll take leave and head home now.'

By the time I reached home, it was evening. Vidyawati ji had just entered the house. She held the pooja *thaali* in her hands.

'Oh you've come. Should I lay the table or would you like some tea first?'

'Tea, please. I'll eat when Papaji comes back.'

'But Bhaiji said he'd come late. There's some function at the college and people have come from outside, so he'll return only after dinner.'

'Oh, that's good in a way. At least he'll be distracted for a while.'

I took the cup of tea and walked into his room. Suddenly I thought of his diary. His study desk had two drawers on either side. I found a fat diary as I opened the very first drawer. It was black and had a frayed binding. Yes, this must be the one. The minute my fingers touched it, the paper rustled. It seemed as if, knowingly or unknowingly, I was about to encroach upon the privacy of Papaji's past memories and his saga. Would it be right? I didn't know. But those moments captured in the documentation were related to my life too.

On the first page were the words, 'For Kamini'.

'Though you have walked out of my life, Kamini, you're etched in my heart exactly as you were the first day we met. Where do I begin? Yes, the wedding! Maybe it was an arrangement of convenience for you. But for me it was like a pilgrimage—an oath—which has just one aim. Nirvana. You forgot, but I remembered all the marriage vows the priest made us ariculate during the ceremony. And the mantra, *Tvan chittam anuchittam bhavatu.* (In the times to come may the harmony of our thoughts be maintained). We had taken each other's hand, tied a knot with a cloth and taken seven steps together—*saptapadi*.

'Kamini, that entire process was imprinted on my heart—perhaps that's why I didn't treat it as a joke, as a means of sexual gratification, but a holy union of two souls. It was an oath to give myself to you completely; a mutual commitment. Arrogance: zero; just a vast sky.

'One of the words from those vows has just come to me, Kamini—*anuchinta*—to know and understand each other's thoughts. But why did you ignore all of it? Why did you never try to understand me or my mind? Maybe because there was a deep financial crisis between us. You were married against your wishes. Such marriages do happen. And people stick to them. I wish you had given me some time. Shailendra had arrived in our life by then to stamp his presence on the marriage.

'But you did not want to emerge from your past ambitions. You wanted to be a fashion designer. I found nothng wrong with that. Every profession has its significance. But you were in too much of a rush. Seeing your beauty fade, you blamed me. I did try my best. I gave tuitions. For your sake I even employed a maid, but you found my silence a weakness, my busyness an inferiority complex. You thought I was an insect trapped in a cocoon. When did you ever understand that my preoccupation was really an exercise in self-development. My spirituality, my fellowship in Psychology were a bore for you. The depth of anything I had couldn't move you even though my love for you defined my identity; it was like a religion for me, Kamini! I wish you had cared to look within once.

'Whenever I came back home I would find Shailendra alone with the maid, crying and kicking. God knows what kind of course you were pursuing. Where did you go? I never asked you because for me trust was paramount...just as it is today. That day when I returned from college, it was rather late. I could see the tracks of the truck and the dragged suitcases. They stared at me accusingly. The whole house rang with a deafening silence. A smoky darkness filled the corners, glaring at me.

'In my hands fluttered the letter of fellowship from the University of Oxford. The pace of achievement just creates an eddy. But I had lost whatever I dreamt of because I lagged way behind, trudging on foot; a home—a home with a small garden in front in which children played. And then I received your letter, Kamini, a letter in which you just offered me some information. It said:

"After deliberating for a long time, I've reached the

conclusion that I cannot live this life in the street with you; it suffocates me. I can see no future for Shailendra here either, Ved, playing *gilli-danda* in the neighbourhood. That's why I sold all my jewellery and got him admitted to Mayo College in Ajmer. At least he'll receive some quality education and lead a decent life. He'll learn the mannerisms I want him to learn. I've deposited the fee for five years. After that he is your responsibility. Along with yours, I'm quitting his life too. Don't even try to look for me, Ved...because the two of us are not made for each other."

'The same day I rushed to Ajmer. My poor six-year-old Shailendra stood there, fearful. I stayed there, close to him, for about ten or fifteen days. I wanted to internalize all the processes and situations. I felt it was best. Maybe for the first time, Kamini's decision regarding Shailedra's future, was right.

'Because she had given me such a precious gift, I forgave her. The imposing building of the school, the atmosphere, the education—if they could steer my son's life in a new direction, I was willing to cooperate. It was my sole aim now to build his future.

'Kamini, wherever you are, accept my gratitude.'

On one page these lines were written in red ink:

You challenged my patience, of which I have enough...

Kamini, I have not given up....

I'm waiting... waiting

With a silent heart
For the moon to become full.

'Kamini, I can wait forever. You have left, but your voice is buried deep within me—the tune that you sometimes hummed ... everything that I could never say, but wanted to. Create something unique for yourself. You have the ability.

March 6

'What happened to me?' I asked, opening my eyes.

'You had a heart attack, Ved Babu.'

Saumitro was staring at me.

'How, Saumitro? Where am I now?'

'At a hospital. Ved Babu...you collapsed while giving a lecture in class. We brought you here in an ambulance. Now you're fine. The crisis is past.'

'Oh.' I don't know whether the crisis had passed or just begun. I lay there quietly, gazing at the white walls for several days...all alone.

Saumitro came in the evenings. That day when he came, he said, 'Yaar Ved, the peon went to your house twice or thrice to look for your wife, but found it locked. When you were in the ICU, your brother came to see you. He mentioned she has left you and that you've moved into an old-age home. You're not all that old—then why?'

Sometimes tears don't come, but the eyes sink in the mire of agony and misery. Maybe I sank into it at that moment.

Saumitro kept me company and looked after me in the hospital. He would come, not my brother or Bhabhi, every second or third day. Truly, a friend is worth much more than one's kith and kin.

I had been unfamiliar with much, but Papaji's diary was familiarizing me with my own family. The broken foundations of our family surfaced as painful scratches upon pieces of paper narrating our history to me. Each past scene appeared like a cinematic experience. Old, forgotten bits and pieces of memory had been kept carefully stored in this document—memories nobody ever spoke of and maybe Shailendra did not even know of. Whenever Papaji was not in the room, and I had time, I would sneak into his room and read his diary.

The other day he was not in his room. In any case, ever since he had become the head of the department his duties had increased.

The page I opened had a peacock feather stuck to it. A colourful feather. And on the opposite page was written:

I wish I were a peacock and could dance in the rain. Kamini would have swallowed my tears—the tears of joy. Someone would have filled her womb again—someone younger than Shailendra ... And I would have roamed the backyard. The house would have felt like a home... *Thumak chalat Ramchandra, baaje paijaniya....*

But where did she have the time? She found my books, my spirituality, and psychology fellowship boring. In her readymade modern world of fashion, names like Freud, Jung and Nietzsche were meaningless. The stars rising on Doordarshan filled her skies. Maybe she was normal. Maybe she was wiser. Maybe I was the one lost—immature. Perhaps that's the way Samsa, the protagonist of *Metamorphosis,* proves his transformation. Kamini too metamorphosed into another being and left for a more colourful, inviting world to make a place for herself, to make a new future—to fulfill her unfulfilled dreams and desires. Maybe by now she has accomplished her goals.

But my knowledge of Psychology says that it is impossible to satisfy the thirst of man. No one has ever been truly satiated, ever.'

After the heart attack, Saumitro had brought me to a guest house where he lived. In the evening, while returning home after our cases, we would have tea together. After that he would either lock himself in his room or, dressed in a white kurta pyjama, leave the house and return late. We would meet the next day at the breakfast table on time. He looked unusually happy and hummed a tune as he polished off his toast and egg, while I would be struggling with the new topic I was supposed to teach.

One day I asked him, 'Yaar, Saumitro, where do you go so late at night? And despite that you manage to take classes the next morning. What's the secret? Let us hear it.'

'Arrey Ved Babu, you will just remain an intellectual.

Bhai, how long will you keep your internal hunger buried inside the pages of these books? I did not marry, but you did. You know better...love, sex...the hunger of the body? Doesn't it trouble you? Don't you ever feel the agony? Why should I hide it from you...it bothers me a great deal...this violent feeling, the violent hunger. I cannot hold back. It's a good market. If you're willing to spend, the most beautiful women are ready to sell themselves.'

He laughed. I was stunned at the conversation. How could he even laugh? But maybe he was lucky. How could someone laugh with such abandon? I couldn't even remember when I had laughed like that the last time.

'Why, what happened? You've gone silent. You must think I'm "cheap" that I'm talking such crap. No, Ved Babu. Telling the truth is not cheap and paid sex is not rape. There's nothing wrong in it and it's safe. Why should I hide it from you?' He squeezed my shoulder and said, 'Why don't you taste it too? Once you get used to it, you won't be able to do without it.'

Then one evening he came and stood at my door.

'Arrey Ved Babu, why do you always look so glum? Get up. Put these books aside and come with me today. It'll be a distraction. Come and see—there exist other arrangements in the world for a person's entertainment and pleasure. Why should you sit like a recluse? Slough off the professor's skin and step out. Come on.'

He took my hand and I allowed myself to be led out. Yes, once in a while one must do something different. With his help I sat in a rickshaw with him. There was an intoxicating smell in his clothes; a sly smile under his moustache. It was a mysterious journey. But I was curious to see where he experienced such heavenly pleasures and brought such abandoned laughter from.

By the end the rickshaw dragged forward. The pace decreased. It was a dark, narrow street and yet well-lit. The crowd edged forward slowly, pushing and jostling. 'Oh, what kind of a place is this, Saumitro?'

'Have you never been here before? You really don't know? And you claim you belong to Agra?'

'No. And if I did, I probably ignored whatever you're telling me now.'

'Arrey, this is a sex market. Look up there—what a sight.' He jerked my head upwards.

There, just above the shops were dilapidated wooden balconies, some painted in gaudy green and orange. On each balcony stood women. I looked carefully. They were making strange signs with their hands and eyes. The conversation continued in sign language between them and the trekkers below.

'See Ved Bhai, what is it called in your language—beauty and grace? Arrey, this is the famous Fulatti Bazaar, Babu. You're supposed to live to the full here; you can even buy pleasure.' Five-hundred rupee notes peeped out of his pocket.

Before I could offer any argument, staggering, with my hand still in his, I climbed a flight of stairs after him. I loosened my legs. I might as well experience this too. It would be interesting to see how bliss was bought and sold in this market.

It was a dirty looking room. I strained my eyes in the faint blue light to see a woman sitting on a mattress on the floor. Some film song was playing on the tape recorder. It didn't sound like music at all; it was alien to my ears. The woman got up, came forward and took Saumitro's hand and mine. She was dressed in a shimmering gold saree and wore a strange perfume.

'Come, Sahibji, what would you like to drink?' The movement of her eyes was strange for me.

'I have brought my drink with me. Just get me a glass?'

Saumitro plonked himself on the floor and I followed him.

'And you?' she came close to me and whispered.

'Ji...anything....' Her skin was visible under her transparent nylon sari. The face had a lot of make up, cheap but inviting. The lips were painted a deep red and a jasmine gajra adorned her hair. If there was any scent in the damp, stale air, it was the jasmine. Intoxicating and dramatic.

A boy brought a glass and ice for Saumitro and he started making a drink. The woman took my hand and leading me said, 'Come, let's give you something else to drink.' I shuddered in her cold grasp, but followed her. In an inner room there was a bed covered with a crumpled sheet.

'Come.' She pushed me.

I fell on the bed, half prone. She switched off the light, removed her sari and slid on top of me. I felt intoxicated by her jasmine gajra maybe for a second. Something stirred within. Her shamelessness was crossing the line when I heard the soft sobbing of a child. The sound shook me. I leapt to my feet and walked out. I saw Saumitro sitting there peacefully, enjoying his drink.

'Oh Saumitro, I'm sorry but I'm leaving. You call this life? Happiness?'

The woman's icy fingers were trying to hold my hand. 'Please come in, Sahib. I'll make you happy.'

'Please,' I said. 'I cannot stand this brazenness.'

'What to say, Sahib. When the wind is strong, you see just one leaf trembling on the branch...hunger; caring for the child. What is shame? We don't know.' She turned and vanished inside the darkness of the room.

I don't know why I felt that the chipped paint on the walls in this room wasn't just crust, but thick sludge that, under the weight of pain and personal conclusions, was falling on me and making me tremble. I walked out quickly and reached the guest house. The whole time I couldn't get rid of that icy touch—a sense of direction that established a balance between body and hunger.

When I came back to the Guest House a magazine lay on the table of the lobby. I ordered some tea, and sipping my tea I turned the pages of the magazine. There were pictures of temples of India. The photographs enhanced their beauty and glorified their old heritage. One page which hit my sensibility displayed the richness of the famous temple of 'Tirupati'. The heaps of currency notes, coins, sparking gold, diamond jewellery were spread on a large carpet and many priest like men were busy counting the money. Another page carried a similar photograph of a Gurudwara, where again many sardars were busy calculating their daily offerings. All the coloured images were dazzling with unusual beauty.

The last photograph...a black and white one was of a young child clad in tattered rags, sitting with an empty bowl near a heap of garbage at a construction site. The caption of the photograph was—"Hunger"

"Sorry...friend we cannot do anything for you, as just now we are to busy making temples, Gurudwaras, and Masjids etc. We have no time."

'Hunger,' I shivered and my emotional strength failed. 'Hunger'—the dark was really so dark yes; today I had encountered 'Hunger', like an emotion...cold and chilling, where hope hung like a solitary leaf on a frail branch of a tree.

Some of my friends planned a trip to Varanasi. Why? Just because it was Dev Deepavali. I had neither been to Varanasi, nor knew what Dev Deepavali was.

Saumitro insisted. I also felt a need for change—a change from my routine. Maybe a dip in the Ganga would provide me some solace. Maybe the historic city of India would throw up a new adventure and infuse the darkness within me with a fresh dream.

We reached Varanasi. After checking into the hotel we went for a sightseeing tour. I was shocked to the core of my heart. What a filthy city, choked with enormous crowds of people of different nationalities. The whole city looked mysterious to me rather than majestic, which is what I was searching for.

When we reached the famous Ghats, they demonstrated another complex aspect of the city. The architecture of some ghats was royal, done by different rulers. But they were ill maintained, fading into gloomy ruins, losing their richness due to the carelessness of its keepers. Several steps led down to the river Ganga. Almost every step was crowded with sadhus and pandits sitting under unique thatched, colourful, umbrellas, exclusive to them.

On some steps were beggars in their threadbare rags, women with shaved heads and skeletal faces. Who were they? Widows in their white sarees, deprived of life—rejected and thrown away like waste. So this was Varanasi...Kashi...the ancient and pious *teerth* of our ancestors?

Those pandits or pujaris were trying to establish eye contact, calling us to pray for our ancestors or ourselves. Their manner reminded me of the seductive women at Fullati Bazaar. Yes, it was no less, but Mishraji and Saumitro sat down upon a platform created by the Pujari. I followed them. The Pujari put a tika of red roli on our foreheads and tied a red thread round our wrists. They even had an old record of family ties, of people who had written their names on it when they visited Kashi. I was not interested in reconnecting with my past. What for?

I walked towards the other side of the ghats where many pyres were choking the air. Human flesh burnt everywhere since people believed that if one made one's last journey to Kashi, one attained moksha. Faith nourishes those who have no wisdom.

The Hindu *Puranas* say Brahma creates, Vishnu maintains and Shiva takes away life. So this city was the abode of Shiva, eager to destroy. And souls waiting to leave their bodies. Millions of them breathed their last on this piece of land. God knew how many. How many hovered over the ghats of the Ganges? How many? But weren't all the souls alike—whether they were of beggars or emperors? I wondered what the well-lit banks of the Ganges would offer them. *Nark* (hell) or *moksha*? What?

'Oh, come on, Mr Philosopher...Ved Babu,' Samumitro

pushed me onto a decorated 'Bajra', an old double-storied boat, which was really mystical. I climbed the rotting wooden steps of our Bajra. There were a few plastic chairs arranged neatly on a cheap carpet so that they did not slip on being moved. The arrangement could not have been better. We sat down on the chairs with boxes of snacks.

'Why is this Dev Deeavali celebrated, Mishraji? And that too after the real Deepavali?' I asked.

'Vedji, as you know, Diwali was first celebrated in Ayodhya when Ramchandraji returned home after having rescued Sitaji from the clutches of Ravana and killing him. Diwali therefore became a reminder of positivity and freedom over negativity and darkness. On Diwali it is always Amavasya—no moon.'

'But today it is Purnima, full moon.'

'Yes, on this particular day, the moon...no, the super moon, is supposed to be closest to the earth, which can bring on a calamity for the inhabitants here. So the devtas decided to celebrate a different kind of Deepavali here in Kashi—by lighting earthen diyas on the Ganges. It was done every year to avoid the evil curses,' Mishraji explained. 'Since then it has been known as Dev Deepavali.'

'It must have been magnificent and majestic those days, but now? Yes, I pity the Ganga. Spirituality and rituals don't suggest destruction and pollution. Look at all these diyas people are floating upon the water.'

'It's an old tradition,' Mishraji wanted to pacify me.

'Prayers are always offered with fire, flowers and the chanting of mantras.'

The diyas either sailed or toppled in the river of gloom. God knows where they were going or for whom. How long could a poor clay lamp burn with crude oil and a wick? Soon it would tip over a wave. A young boy stood with a few diyas upon a *thali*.

Balbir said, 'Ved, you should also light one. Set it afloat in the river. It will fulfill your wish, your dreams. It will sing a new song for the days still to come.'

He descended the stairs of the Bajra to step closer to the river to float his own diyas.

'No,' I pulled my hand back when the boy with the *thali* approached me. 'No, I don't want to choke the already over-polluted river.'

I returned to my chair. The full moon of Purnamasi reflected in the water. The light penetrated inside to heal the heart of the aching river. Or perhaps it tried to brighten the Ganges with its own light.

Soon the diyas were extinguished...gone. The flowers sank. But the moon was constant. Its light had a firm message: illumination from within; to be bright and awake inside and then move outwards.

May 7

Freud believed that outside of himself, in the world, a person either sought a mirror image of his mother or of his father in other people. However, in the modern day atmosphere the meaning of relationships has altered. They are cruel and tense. The thought of relatives leaves a bitter taste in the mouth. At least in my case I have always received a cold shoulder and bitterness from them. I don't even want to remember those painful experiences, but it isn't so easy to forget either.

The other day my student Natasha came and stood next to me when I was going through one such miserable phase. Her words are so sweet. And she is so simple—not just simple but gracious. As she walked in carrying her books I felt as though a gust of cool breeze had stealthily blown in. I turned around suddenly, wondering whether I had switched on the air conditioner somehow, but no, it was off. The refreshing coolness came from her body. I don't know why I felt the saree she wore was less of a saree and more of a prayer flag hoisted during the pooja. It felt sacred. With her arrival the room was filled with a strange light—something I had never experienced before.

Many times in college when Achla Awasthi happens to cross my path she deliberately lets her pallu slide. Whenever she says hello with those lips painted with a dark red lipstick I find it disgusting. And there are other colleagues—Mrs

Rehman, Tulika Rai—always busy trying to ensnare men. Many times in the staff quarters, Purvi Mathur from the neighbourhood would knock at the door in a thin, transparent nightie. Sometimes, she would say, 'Please have some cake. I've baked it myself,' and sometimes she would say, 'I brought you some coffee I made'. That's why I had to leave that house and I moved into a senior citizens' home. Here everybody's been plucked out of their lives and thrown into forced solitude and loneliness. I too am one of them—alone, lonely....But yes, I have books. A university job. And my students come over sometimes to give me company.

But this girl Natasha comes researching human emotions. She talks to everyone. She collects case histories. She awakes emotions in them. Flowing with the tide she is a tiny bud who is yet to grow into a flower.

May 20

Kamini left me also because she wanted that in my loneliness and the utter silence within I should discover the truth of my own existence. And then the loving moments I had spent with her were so powerful that I never really got over them. Perhaps they became the reason behind my physical abstemiousness. That is why, even amidst a horde of women and their bedlam, I could steer my single-wheeled chariot forward without a scratch. When I think of it now I want to pat myself on the back. She rose above the situation and moved forward. She wanted to climb up the ladder with her industriousness to reach her own truth. One must not fear any obstacles—neither worldly ties nor social norms or even religion. I'm sure she must have achieved the ambition that had always throbbed in her heart.

And then I see Vidyawati Behen at the Home. What horrifying and disgusting experiences she has been through, and yet, amazingly, she never allows it to show but keeps herself busy caring for other people. She has filled the gaping hole in my heart in the shape of a sister.

And now Shailendra and Natasha's presence has pervaded the house like pleasant music. Her arrival has infused not only Shailendra's life with meaning, but mine too. She is not really fussy, yet has a palpable femininity about her. Everything has changed with her arrival—the taste of food, the scent of the house....I never knew before that the air within the house had a fragrance. And yes I sleep well on mattresses and linen Shailendra and Natasha have chosen this time. I spent a long period of twenty or twenty-five years on my own in a rented room. Life was not worthwhile. Just passing the time seemed a punishment. But now I feel like planting some flowers in the garden so that they bloom and endorse the fact that this is my home. Home—where life has got back meaning—meaning that was lost the day Kamini dragged her luggage out of the house.

After reading Papaji's diary I sat in pin-drop silence for a while. It was a documentation of his most personal experiences. Everything that he could not share with anybody, that he had never been able to confess to anybody. Thousands of experiences, crises, his loneliness and the hermit-like life emerging from it—it was all there in the diary.

I kept thinking about how well-known he was for his knowledge and wisdom, what a high position he held, how he was respected at the university and yet he had never made any show of it; there was no burnished nameplate, no desire for anything. Why had he trudged on in the desert like this—neither complaining of the heat, nor expressing any wish to be enveloped in the cool moonlight. How had he survived? Though he could have taken the highway he had opted for a narrow, dusty path and carried on with the same kind of sincerity, simply for the sake of sharing or gaining knowledge—the path of experimentation and research. In spite of the fact that he had to swallow the reality of his life as a bitter pill. There were so many students like me whom he had taught for free. He imposed no conditions but did his job with a warm smile—and the smile spoke of his self-satisfaction. In fact, I became friends with him due to such 'emotions'. The emotions began to gain depth, so much so that I drowned in them. So now, I would have to learn from him how to be complete in a world of nothingness.

I bumped into Mandira in the hospital corridor.

'Oh Natasha, how are you? I came to see you. Tell me, how is Shailendra's treatment getting on?'

'Mandira!' I hugged her. She too put her arms around me. Right then I needed that kind of warm, sympathetic touch.

'What a crisis you're facing... and Shailendra? Any improvement? Come, let's sit in the coffee shop.'

'It's been almost eight or nine months, Mandira. Forget about me, but Shailendra is in a lot of pain. To tell you the truth I don't see anything getting better. And the doctors —more than Shailendra they're trying to give me strength. They feel Shailendra is on his death bed, but I cannot believe it—but then...the world runs on faith, doesn't it?'

The coffee arrived. Maybe even Mandira had no words for me.

'Okay...you tell me, Mandira, your artist friend, Zafar, how is he? Is he with you these days or...?'

'No, Natasha. He's in Jhansi. He's painting the ruins

there. He feels these archeological ruins too have soul, and that by giving them shape and structure you can revive them.'

'He's an artist after all. Artists tend to live in their own world.'

'Perhaps that's why he forgets that I'm waiting for him. There something such as the real world.? Me...Love.'

'Is your live-in relationship working well? Your dad? Has he agreed to your wedding or not?'

'No, Natasha. He's inflexible. Because he just doesn't like Zafar. An artist. Blasé. And then Muslim. He finds it ridiculous that I love him, but I cannot help it. It doesn't matter if the wedding doesn't happen. We love each other and live together. That is enough. It has a charm of its own. We'll carry on like that as long as we can.'

'But artists are not carefree any more, Mandira. These days Indian artists are quite renowned the world over. Sculptures and paintings have become so expensive....'

'That's true. It's not about money; it's a matter of habit. His last exhibition was quite successful. The bank balance is good. And I too have a job. Bought a new flat two months ago. But his habits—what does one do about them? The things he's crazy about. They take him on a new adventure every time. These days he's roaming around ruins. He thinks his painting them gives them a new life. Every rock becomes a face and talks to him. He's even writing a book on it.'

'Oh really?'

'Spoke to him this morning. He said he'd be back this weekend. If he comes I'd like you to come down on Sunday. I want you to meet him. Okay, Natasha....'

'I cannot commit, Mandira. And then Sundays are busy too. I'm taking an intensive dietician's course, so a lot of charts etc. need to be prepared.'

'When did you start that?'

'It's been about two or three months. Papaji attends to Shailendra in the evenings, so I can go for my classes. The Tragedy has altered the times. And there are financial problems. How long can Papaji manage alone? Besides, he's just been appointed as vice principle, so his duties have multiplied. I need to give him space. Shailendra is my responsibility too after all.'

'Then what about your research? The thesis you were writing...?'

'I'm doing that alongside. I think I should be able to finish in a month or two.'

'Then what about your future?'

'Mandira...Shailendra, God know when he'll recover. A month...two months...a year? I took up the dietician's course so that I could stay close to him. The hospital will offer me a job. I'll balance work and caring for him.'

'Don't you feel suffocated here? How can you breathe in this environment of constant pain and death?'

'I have already lost my identity, Mandira. I don't

remember what I was; I don't know what I've become.'

'You have become extremely strong, Natasha ji. You have transformed into a very good human being.' God knows where Harry suddenly appeared from.

Startled, Mandira looked at him. She was astonished at his twisted body structure and drooling mouth.

'Mandira, this is Harry,' I said. 'A special male nurse here. He's very kind and looks after the patients really well.' Holding his hand I said, 'Harry, how did you say such a nice thing about me?

I was amazed.

'You know Dr Prashant Chapekar, the psychiatrist who gives electric shocks to that Muslim patient? He was saying it to Dr Sandeep. I heard him. Why? Is there something wrong?'

'No, no, nothing's wrong. You can never say anything wrong. Go to Pooja. She needs you.'

'Okay.' He scampered off.

'Who is this strange creature?'

'You'll be surprised, Mandira. He's a Down's Syndrome survivor. He was born with this condition, but overcame his circumstances to such an extent that he's completed his nursing course. He cares for patients here. He's a very good human being. There's a teenage girl here who'd gone into depression after rape. To a great extent, his efforts have helped to revive her. He has been looking after patients selflessly and has helped many to recover well.

Mandira squeezed my hand tightly. 'Be brave.' There was nothing else left to say. I walked into Dr Sandeep's clinic.

'Yes, Natasha?' He turned towards me.

'Sir, may I sit down? Do you have a few minutes to spare?'

'Yes, please take a seat.'

'Sir, it's been almost fourteen months. What future does Shailendra have? Can't some doctor be called from abroad to take a look at him? There must be some new treatment. Slowly he's turning into a vegetable. He can barely speak now. If I say something he can only blink. He cannot move his hands. And so many bed sores, blood....' My patience had begun to run out.

Dr Sandeep stayed silent for a while. Then he stood up and put his hand on my shoulder. 'Be prepared, Natasha,' he said.

'For what?' Neither was he willing to spell it out, nor was I willing to hear it. Yes, even silence can convey a lot—that which words sometimes fail to do. To change the subject he said, 'I heard you've completed your dietician's course?'

'Yes, thanks to you, and Rajnarayan ji. Just sitting on the steel bench night and day I would have turned into steel myself, but for you both. Before that could happen you showed me a way out. You made me human, made me a dietician. I will never forget this favour, sir. Another thing, sir, I've completed my thesis. I plan to submit it soon.'

'How much you manage to do—caring for patients, studying, doing your course and thesis...I admire you, Natasha.' He handed me a packet. 'Take it. It's a book I have brought for you. It's Osho. I like the philosophy and the writing style. No, it is not spirituality; don't misinterpret it, but his religion sounds like poetry that strikes a cord with you. It will ease your doubts and questions.'

At that moment Pooja arrived with Harry. She was looking absolutely fine now. A floral top over tight jeans looked good on her.

'Arrey Pooja, you look very nice. I believe you're going home tomorrow?' I gave her a warm embrace.

'Yes, Didi. I just came to tell you that I'm going home finally—but I'll never forget you all. All of you are so kind. And my mother? I hate her. How terribly she's behaved. I dread going home; I don't know how she'll treat me....'Her voice broke.

'You are very brave, Pooja.' Dr Sandeep patted her gently.

'But Doctor, I don't know what my future will be like? I'm scarred. My mother says I've ruined the name of the family. And I don't know how my friends will behave when I return to school.' She began to cry. 'I don't know what will happen to me.'

'Arrey, Pooja, don't cry. Whatever happened was not your fault. And then a mother is a mother. She will take care of everything. Don't cry, please. Nothing will happen. All will be well. Don't worry.'

'Didi, even my name isn't mine anymore. I have even lost my identity,' she wept. 'What have I become?'

Harry took her hand. 'No, Pooja, no. You must not cry. Come, we'll play carom.' He led her away.'

'Life is strange, Natasha. It's a peculiar journey. And being a doctor is a very big test for a human being. One sees so much. I don't know how Pooja's parents will handle her life.'

'Her mother is very negative. If you say anything, she begins to shout and scream. Being the mother, at least she should have helped Pooja. Had she been more supportive her daughter would have recovered much faster. But her attitude towards life is peculiar.'

'Not everybody is like you, Natasha. You've spent so much time in the hospital constructively, making the best of a bad situation. Who knows how to utilize time better than you?'

His phone was constantly ringing so he stood up and looked at me. 'Sorry, Natasha, I have to go.'

He turned around and left. A dreadful silence followed. I pulled the book out of the packet. The title sent a shiver down my spine: *Until I Die*.

The page my trembling fingers had stopped at read, "Death and sex are two sides of the same coin. What sex unites death separates. If sex is synthetic, death is analytic. Sex synthesizes, death analyzes. The act is the same."

Oh, how could Osho say the act is the same? One is an unparalleled act of pleasure, a sweet moment in life, which one wants to live and relive. And the other shakes my soul with its footsteps.

Oh...where did I drop the black thread Amma had tied around my neck? When did it break? Where did it fall? And if it did, how come I did not notice?

Some Pir Baba had tied a ray of hope in a black knot round my neck—a reason for my mother's faith. When the knot breaks faith is lost. But one still had to learn how to live.

Outside the hospital too it was getting dark. In winters, the darkness arrives before the evening hour. Time embraces it eagerly. And I had been avoiding this darkness for a long time.

The fruit shop was right in front of me. I asked the rickshaw-wala to stop and climbed down to buy some. The shopkeeper was coughing badly as though he had had a fit. His helplessness made me pause; I forgot what I had to buy. Which fruit? What did I like? I just couldn't remember that Shailendra and Papaji liked papayas and Vidyawatiji liked apples. I handed the fellow my water bottle. Shailendra doesn't even cough any more. My life hangs over him now. What momentum, what energy had managed to drag me here?

'What would you like?' The seller had managed to regain control over his bout of coughing.

'Anything...a papaya, a kilo of apples. And listen—I hope you're taking the tablets I got you. Your cough hasn't improved at all.'

'Yes, behenji, I'm better than before. Thanks to you I got a check-up done at the hospital. They diagnosed the problem. The medication is working. I can sleep properly at night.' He handed me the packets.

The rickshaw had started moving. There was hardly any crowd on the road. Some children, men and women were sleeping on the pavement on newspapers. Some were yawning behind blankets. The women could hardly conceal their aging, ravaged bodies, but busied themselves warming their hands over a fire. It was only seven in the evening. It wasn't really all that cold. What meaning did these garbage dumps offer to their lives? A terrible stench rose in the air. I covered my nose with my dupatta, wondering how these people could sleep in a place like this. There were mosquitoes swarming over the drains, dogs foraging for food in the trash heaps, mice ... and yet they continued to sleep. More than them I pitied the poor road. It needed more rest than they did; needed to be rid of the coughs, needed peace. When would it ever get it? Freedom from her muddy sorrow?

Darkness was fast spreading. Night was upon us. It would envelop everybody—the travelers, the pedestrians, the lame beggar, the wheezing shopkeeper, the animals and insects in the drain...because darkness was deep and black—so deep that it could swallow all.

I had just read it. There was a line by Rumi in the book Sandeep Sir had given me: 'Darkness is never absolute'. The thick darkness was unique. What would happen to the moon's rush of emotions? What terrible things the poor earth had to face. Even the sky had gone silent at its pitiable condition. It couldn't take it. Maybe that's why the moonlight was pale, its emotions turbulent...?

When I stepped out after my viva, Professor Balbir and Dr Manav were waiting in the corridor. I waved a greeting and tried to leave quietly, but they stopped me.

'Arrey, Natasha, we are very impressed with your thesis. Indeed, you have acquainted us very diligently with the worldly, egoist mind and feelings and brought it to the point where the ego loses its identity and a new door is opened to the self. A self brightened with the light to emotions, which cannot be divided into parts—id, ego and superego. It's very difficult to establish such individuality where mind, body and soul make one complete human being. Where do you find them in the real world?'

'Sir, human beings haven't become so aimless yet! Even amidst worldly ambitions a man can live with his head held high.' Papaji arrived just then.

'Congratulations, Natasha. The sacred fire you've been feeding for sometime has finally had its last offering today. Everyone was praising the pattern of your research—how you've combined the worldly and religious boundaries to give a new definition to the mind. I am very proud of you.'He patted my head.

'Ved ji, you should send this research to Yale University. They are going to have a seminar on 'Emotions.' You never know, it may be selected,' Professor Balbir suggested.

'Okay, I will do that.'

And I don't know how I had steered away from the world of books and lost myself in a world of relationships. Where everything was deceptive and full of fraud, which had taken away my sense of self. What had I become? Bankrupt, emotionally spent, a statue falling apart. Natasha? Now it was for me to decide whether I should stay in this world where every moment was a challenge, or in the hospital as a dietician where problems were living creatures. Treatment meant depending on somebody else. Man was paradoxical; nature distorted....

It was a small function. Dr Rajnarayan handed me my dietician's certificate. There were some other candidates in the assembly like me. The whole process had given me new confidence and inspired a resolution in me to begin life anew. Now I would be financially empowered and be able to help Papaji in this long, painful journey Shailendra had to take.

Everybody was busy in the celebrations, enjoying tea, but I was in a hurry. I wanted to rush to Papaji and Shailendra and acquaint them with my little achievement that I was now a qualified dietician.

It was late. But then it would usually be late by the time I finished. It was 7.30 pm. I had to leave. As I stepped out of the campus I felt it was a special day. Maybe a festival? Yes, perhaps the city was celebrating Diwali. But my festivals? I seemed to be standing at the brink of something unknown.

Today was a day of achievement. That itself made it festive. Filled with conflicting thoughts and doubts I stopped a rickshaw and reached the hospital.

Out of the hazy darkness in the corridor a figure emerged—the Muslim friend. His mother was happy. She grabbed my arm and said, 'Oh, where were you, beta? I was looking for you. Sahil is alright now; you will have to visit us at our place now.'

'Aunty, congratulations. It's a happy day for you.' Then I took Sahil's hand and said, 'Good. You've got rid of your troubles. Now you should start your life afresh. Go home.'

But Sahil looked at me strangely. It was a look he had never had before. Then he said, 'Yes, we are going. We are going.' Then he turned and said, in an unusual poetic manner:

'I have been to that heavenly garden;
Sometimes before the spring; sometimes after.'

There was a twinkle in his eye. 'Did you go, Sister?'He caught my hand and said, 'I have visited that glorious garden many times—the one you describe as my home...before the spring and after. But now that abode of love and compassion, which was full of flowers, is filled with dry leaves....There is unending autumn.'

'Come, the car has come.' His mother detached his hand from mine roughly and dragged him away. She left and so did he, but the memories and thoughts remained. Memories and thoughts that fester old abscesses, that return again and again to haunt you. What is happening now at this moment will be past tomorrow.

Sister Dorothy had arrived. 'Happy Diwali, Natasha.' She took out a laddoo from the box in her hand and offered it to me. 'Have it. Pooja's father sent them. Harry too is happy. Pooja has gone home. She tied him a rakhi before leaving. Isn't that good news?'

In the deep darkness of the Diwali evening, it was like seeing a beautiful diya light up. Though the light was faint, it brightened the entire corridor. Before the carvings of the gods on the walls, the clay idols of Lakshmi-Ganesh had been propped upon a stool, adding to the significance of the festival. The place was strewn with flowers. Lighted candles stood in rows. A box of sweets lay nearby with *kheele-bataashe*. Patients from all religions—doctors, nurses... cradling their sorrows, lost in their own thoughts stood there as someone sang the aarti and devotional songs of Diwali.

Papaji and I stood facing each other. Between us Shailendra lay unconscious. And both of us seemed like mirrors placed opposite each other. When you witness imperfections and understand situations, it is called psychology. You realize that your life too is transitory and imperfect—where there is neither light nor fire. It is like a weak lamp which refuses to be lit. It cannot, even if it wants to. Its flame isn't a flame but a fading glow...like Shailendra's life. Why does the fuel finish so soon? Lack of thought fills the time.

As I opened the door to Shailendra's room and went in, I stood in shock. The bed was empty. The sheets were never so deserted, so crumpled, so white and colourless. The glucose bottle hanging from the stand, the rubber tubes, falling droplets stared at me.

'Shailendra! Shailendra!' I rushed to the ICU and

found an almost unconscious Papaji sitting on a chair in a terrible state.

'Papaji! Papaji!' I had to shake him awake. 'What happened? Are you alright?'

He opened his eyes and gestured with a finger. Opposite, through a transparent glass door, I could see doctors and nurses rushing here and there.

'What's going on?'My legs collapsed under me. 'Is anybody there? Tell me, how's my Shailendra?' My patience ran out.

Sister Dheera appeared. 'Natasha, control yourself.'

I watched carefully. Shailendra lay on his side. He had not even turned on his own for so many months. Then why today? I couldn't see any more since the doctors crowded around him.

The night passed. It was daylight. And then afternoon. But the suffocating darkness remained. Who was covering Shailendra with my white dupatta? What was this? A gust of wind touched my face. The time of day seemed impossible to tell—what hour was it? Was it morning or evening?

'Papaji! Papaji!' Recovering my wits I brought Sister Dheera over and said, 'Please take care of him; he is a heart patient.'

'Okay, Natasha. You be brave.' She made him take a medicine. Harry brought some water. A new nurse brought some sandwiches. 'Please have them.' She tried to force-feed him. 'You've been sitting around like this for so long. You haven't even had a sip of water.' She slipped a Sorbitrate tablet under my tongue too, along with Papaji. Protest?

I broke into a sweat. My body tingled. There was hardly any sensation left. 'Papaji, control yourself. I'll go inside and see how Shailendra is doing. Sister...Dr Sandeep is busy operating, isn't he? Why hasn't he stepped out? Why hasn't he told me anything?'

I opened the door to the ICU and went in. My bangles jingled loudly for no reason in the heavy silence. Dr Sandeep was busy, but did not meet my eyes. Shailendra still lay on his side, unmoving.

Dr Prashant...Dr Sandeep...had removed the mask from his face. Sister Dorothy was cleaning his face with cotton wool. Like a few words left unsaid a few bubbles had collected around his mouth. Sister closed his eyes.

'No, Sister. Please let him see. See Shailendra, I've worn a colourful sari today...and bangles too. Didn't you say I shouldn't look like a student? That's why I'm wearing all these. Come on, get up. Look at me....'

His stony stare, lifeless pupils were lost in themselves... turned away from reality, from me, from Papaji, from all ties—and from all physical pain. The moment trembled as though in a cold snowstorm in a Himalayan cave. Lightning struck.

'Come Natsha.' Sister Elena tried to bring me back to the present. 'He is no more.'

So Shailendra had gone. Through closed doors, breaking away from the grasp of airtight windows, he had left.

'Come. You are brave. Face the situation. Shailendra is dead.'

Who had spoken such bitter words?

A curtain over the drama of life. The tall, impregnable barriers, the white walls were free of emotion—bare, silent. Nothing, nobody counted. Could somebody be so senseless?

'Here, have some water. Don't know how long you've been thirsty.' Somebody offered me a glass. What did he know about thirst? No, I would not cry. Somebody brought me outside. I thought I would see the horizon...notice something new...but the steel bench that had been my companion for a year or more was left behind.

Maybe someone was waiting outside the hospital somewhere? But clouds had gathered in the sky. Even the heavens were crying. But I would not cry. Somebody was shaking me. 'Face the reality, Natasha. Look, his body's been loaded in the ambulance.'

Someone pushed him in the ambulance. Out of the white cloth wrapped around the body a hand fell out. I had held this hand just the day before. Why were the lines on his palm so faded? It was a bare, empty hand... cold, lifeless.

'Come, we've reached home.'

'Home?'

'Yes.'

Papaji and I looked at each other as if seeing each other for the first time.

Papaji's friends had arrived—Dr Rajnath, Saumitro, Baba, Amma, Urvashi. Vidyawatiji was managing the situation well.

Avoding everybody's eye, I slipped into my room and crouched in a corner as though shrivelled. I had never had a proper sleep, the sleep that gives rise to pleasant dreams. I had only managed to brighten my darkest nights through the medium of books. But now—there would be no waiting, no effort, no excitement...nothing.

When agony crossed all limits of endurance...in this state of consciousness a body was just a body. Amma was howling away, pulling me in an embrace. Mandira took her away.

Dr Sandeep also stood there. 'Come, Natasha, let's finish the rituals. Come on, get up.'

'Get up.'

The pyre was lit holding Papaji's hand. I finished the last rituals of the body I had loved so much. Then we returned home amidst the dying relationships that Vidyawatiji had somehow kept going. The fire and smoke from Shailendra's body was still palpable around me.

Amma continuously cried, 'Oh, my poor child suffered someone's evil eye. How will she live now?'

'Poor child.'

It struck me like a nail. 'I'm not a poor, pitiable creature. Please Amma, stop it.'

'Yes. Didi is brave,' said Urvashi. 'Didi has always been like a lamp post, lighting up other people's lives, guiding them. Amma, don't say such things. Stay quiet. Let her get a grip on herself.'

She held me as though I were shards of broken glass.

'Okay. Come Urvashi. Get her to change her clothes. Pull out a white sari and get her dressed. The neighbourhood women are about to come and Shailendra's tai too.'

'No Amma, I won't be able to do anything. Whatever I'm wearing is fine. I cannot put up a pretence. Please, just leave me alone.'

'Come on, there is something called worldliness? These are ancient customs. You must oblige, beta. Come...' She removed the colourful bangles from my arms which I wore to please Shailendra.

'Leave her alone, Amma,' Urvashi tried to reason with her. 'What's wrong with this sari? You go ahead; I will bring her.'

Mandira came. We stood facing each other. In a complex situation, it was a tentative decision. But Mandira and only Mandira knew my inner state.

Outside in the verandah a carpet had been spread out. Papaji sat in front of Shailendra's photo with his eyes closed. I had settled down next to Amma and Baba. A large, fat, unknown woman stepped forward and cried, 'Oh Bahurani, you're already a widow in your youth. How will you survive now for the rest of your life...?'

'Please sit down.' Mandira freed me from her stifling grasp.

'Oh, let me express my condolences. I'm Shailendra's tai. When his mother wasn't at home I used to feed him....'

'That's alright. Sure you must have done a lot. Your pain is great. But what can one do now?'

Taiji sat down. Different expressions of sorrow, true and false, emerged. As though someone was trying to squeeze out oil from sand. It was a performance and a reality—partly natural, partly dramatic.

'Arrey Papaji, why are you sitting on the ground? Your knees hurt so terribly. Mandira, please help him to a chair.' I could not bear his broken, shattered persona. No, I could not allow him to return to the environment of the old age home. What did I have to do with these passive, illogical, statements and the different opinions of different people? I arranged a chair for Papaji and made him sit down on it.

I brought a tape recorder from inside the house and played a bhajan tape Papaji used to listen to daily: '*Allah tero naam, Ishwar tero naam ... sabko sanmati de bhagwan...*'

Taiji wiped her crocodile tears. Leaving Papaji, she moved towards Amma and put a hand upon her shoulder. 'God,' she glared at me as she spoke, 'the girls these days...'

Just then Sardar Uncle and Devaki ji from *Simran* arrived. Behind them entered a man with boxes full of food. I stood up and asked them to take the chairs.

Being practical, Papaji said, 'Yes, Bhaiji, you have come from so far off?'

'How could I not come, Bhai Saab....? Natasha *baliye*, you're like Simran to me. And then I was there when your marriage was fixed. The wedding celebrations happened at *Simran*.' Old memories flowed out of his eyes as tears. Taking my hand he began to weep.

Devaki aunty kept patting my back. Then she asked Mandira, 'Has anybody eaten or not? Come beta, serve the food to everybody. I made the gulab jamuns myself.'

When nobody got up I said, 'Thank you, aunty. You remembered what I like and what I don't. I had forgotten.' Mustering courage I gave the boxes to Mandira and my sister. 'Urvashi, serve the food to everybody. Devaki aunty has been so kind to bring it for us.'

'Oh God, this woman isn't affected by the passing away of her husband at all! At the time of sorrow all she can think of is kachori-samosa.' Turning to Amma she said, This is what you've taught your daughter? That's why they say one should investigate a family background before bringing a girl from it, but who listens to me? Who ever did?'

Amma took my hand and said, 'Bitto, sit down. Urvashi, Mandira...put these things inside.'

'Amma...'

'Sit down. Quiet now.' Amma pushed me to sit down again.

That day when I came into the room Papaji wasn't there. Maybe he had gone out early. Usually he would sit on the bench in the garden and have his tea and even take a walk, but that day the tea cup was only half empty and he wasn't around. Vidywatiji mentioned he had left to meet someone. I went into his room to clean up and saw his diary lying there. He had forgotten to lock it safely in his drawer. For me it was an opportunity to peep into his heart.

It said—"It always pleased me to travel to the hills. I was infatuated with the solid rocks. Climbing up was a challenge. Whenever Shailendra came down for his vacations we would go either to Simla or to Mussoorie. It was a precious time for me.

Those times were like turning a new page with Shailendra. When he had ice cream I remembered what it was to taste something sweet. He loved Chinese food. I would watch in amazement as he wolfed down his slippery noodles using two thin wooden sticks he called chopsticks. And I struggled to have them even with a fork. Such experiences were new for me...and I was living for Shailendra. In Mussoorie, he insisted on staying at hotel Savoy. His friends from the royal family stayed there. Staying there was also an experience—an introduction to sophistication. I remember a line from Charlie Chaplin: 'Don't shut love out of your life by saying it's impossible to find.'

Once Shailendra and I went to Kufri. For the first time I saw the peaks covered with a blanket of snow. We played with snowballs and slipped on the snow. There were several white birds there too. When they flew, it seemed as if a part of a cloud was flying. When they sat in a corner, they seemed a part of the ice. Suddenly, a bird with blue feathers hopped over and sat down amongst them. The others began to flirt with it. Trying to escape them she ran from there and landed upon my open palm. She had probably found the roughness enticing. Maybe that's why it scratched a prayer upon it with its beak and then flew away. The next day I went that way again and sat and waited for that bird—the white ones were also looking for it—but it did not appear. God knows where it vanished. The way Kamini disappeared with all the colours of my life, erasing her vows and signatures. But on my palm her scratches, the language her tiny feet had etched, her message—all were alive. I don't know if it was hypnotism or a farewell song or a parting message. In the seclusion of the Himalayas—a subtle warning?

But ever since Natasha has arrived in this house I've begun to feel that that little blue bird was actually a symbol of sweetness that warmed our otherwise cold lives. She is so different from Kamini. Devoid of arrogance, simple and straightforward, so respectful towards me—maintaining the balance between managing Shailendra and me so well.

I was amazed at how when Shailendra was in such pain she could be mentally so strong, endure everything with such single-minded, resolute focus—like trying to walk on the edge of a knife. She managed to juggle her studies and caring for her husband equally well.

Today, I hold myself responsible. I'm guilty when it comes to Natasha. I was the one who asked her to come into our lives. And she did. Saumitro was the one who once told me, 'Women have a supernatural ability to know what is happening in a man's soul.' Who could know about their mental make up better than he?

But I am ashamed today. I ruined a nice young woman's life. What are four or five years of a married life? How well she had jelled with Shailendra after the wedding; how she had turned this house into a home in the one year they spent here. I did not expect it, given that she came from not a very well-to-do family, but she blossomed so well. But now after such a tragic incident I cannot see her wilted like this. With Shailendra, I have lost everything. I'm a broken man.

Maybe this is my destiny. And in this mire I am gathering layers of agony. Look at Javed Akhtar on television echoing my sentiment:

Tumse bichad kar zinda hun,
Jaan, bahut sharminda hun.
(How am I alive after your departure?
My dearest, I am ashamed of myself.)

Vidyawati Behen was singing an *aarti*. She usually sang bhajans in her room in the evenings. Once when I asked she said, 'It is about having attained God; it is a hymn of happiness.' But today she is singing *Tera tujhko arpan, kya laage mera...*'

But me—I have lost everything; been robbed of everything. I had stitched it all together industriously with each breath in my body. When did I ever want to surrender it willingly? Shailendra lost his life. All the frenzied running around, all the travels, all knowledge—nothing helped.

My poor soul has been wandering through so many lifetimes—just to bear these punishments? Why does one suffer so many curses, such retribution in a single lifetime? And then Natasha...so pure and innocent...why did she have to face such awful trials? What kind of a river-shaped life is this that has swallowed all my diyas? All the light, all the wicks, all the oil has been sucked into a deep, dark abyss.

It was evening and getting darker by the hour. Papaji still had not returned home. After Shailendra's death both of us had immersed ourselves in our work. Maybe it was also a fact that we were avoiding each other. When we met, we would just make small talk. I tried my best to keep him happy. I made sure his favourite dishes were served, but every day he was eating less and less. Why was he punishing himself? We all had suffered enough. Now we made friends with our suffering.

Did his late return home have something to do with his growing friendship with Saumitro uncle? No, I couldn't afford to think on those lines.

I slipped into the veranda and stepped over the tiles to the platform around the tree and sat down. I don't know after how many weeks or days I had come here; how Shailendra and Papaji loved to sit here and have their tea. But now neither Papaji nor I ever sat here. Even consolatory messages and words sound false because death is a consequence. One accident. And the end is nothingness.

Yes, it was a consequence both of us had to endure and make up for this lack in our lives in some other way. Even to think of it was so difficult. But Papaji could contemplate it much better than I could.

I looked towards the sky. There was a full moon and a star was also visible. One. Just one. Maybe it was a transfiguration of Shailendra. Maybe that's why a jet could fly so easily between the moon and that star. A long trail of smoke, like a partitioning line, hung in the air. On one such aircraft I had traveled to Singapore with Shailendra—a land of dreams. God knows what terrible curse erased it so heartlessly. But could it really be expunged? In the darkness within sometimes light rises as the sun and fills me. But the truth...? The mind knows and understands, but the body? The body is at war with itself.

This partitioning line between the stars and the moon was perhaps trying to tell me that a journey was not simply a journey. It was a journey of self-actualization. It was a progress towards recognizing oneself, a research upon the self.

The gate opened and Papaji stepped inside. I followed him in. I wanted to see him.

'Arrey, you're still awake, Natasha?'

'I was waiting for you. Papaji, why do you come back so late?'

'Did you need me for something?' He was avoiding my eyes again. Picking up his bag and the pile of papers he started towards his room.

'Papaji, I'm serving dinner. Please come to the table.'

'You still haven't eaten, Natasha?'

'How could I?' I had to break my silence. I had to give vent to the lava boiling inside.

For some time the sound of our cutlery at work echoed in the silence. Then I could not restrain myself.

'Papaji, today you will have to tell me why you're drifting away from me. Have I inconvenienced you in some way? Did I commit some crime?' I could not hold back my tears.

'Arrey beta, please don't cry. You're my one and only anchor for whom I want to live. But Natasha...I feel guilty. You married Shailendra upon my insistence. At that time I felt that your presence in our lives would sweeten all the previous bitterness. But the dreams shattered. I never expected Shailendra would leave us like this. Man proposes, God...'

In the darkness two tear stained faces stared at each other; yet the pain could not drain out.

'Papaji, please have some water.' I needed to regain composure.

'Natasha, I've been trying to muster courage for days now to say this to you.' Then with great effort he said, 'Beta, I think you should remarry. Whoever you wish; whoever you like. I will do your *kanyadaan* as your father. Please, Natasha.' He put his hand upon mine soaked with tears.

'Papaji, how could you even think such a thing? Why can't I live here with you as your daughter? You already know I wasn't ready for marriage even earlier. Whatever the circumstances...karma or positive energy...I just felt myself drawn to Shailendra's life and yours. And now once again....'

'Natasha, all my friends—even Dr Sandeep, Saumitro, Rajnarayan—have been suggesting that I should get you married. It's my responsibility, beta. After that....'He turned away to wipe the tears his eyes.

'What after that?'

'Rajnarayan's brother has invited me to work at Edinburgh University. It's a job offer. He stays there alone. I've been thinking I should go—go far away. I'm exhausted. All the lamps have extinguished, Natasha. It's pitch dark now and it's suffocating. He slunk down upon a chair. I don't know if I helped him or myself....'Papaji, you must go. You need a break.'

I stood up in the silence. It was as though someone had placed dead weight upon me. A strange kind of shiver ran down my spine. Oh Papaji, what did you just say? My head began to spin. The thought of losing my support system caused an internal turmoil.

'Beta, I'm sorry. I just blabbered in a rush. We don't need to take any decisions in haste. Mull over it all you need before you decide. Don't be offended. You're intelligent, Natasha. I'm your father first; your guardian later.'

I don't know how long we sat there lost in the haze of our thoughts before Vidyawatiji came and switched the light on in my room. 'Arrey, how long will you people sit here in the dark like this? Come out.'

I thought about how we would have survived had Vidyawati ji not been around.

In the distance we could hear a voice singing a sweet

song. We didn't know who it was. The song seemed to be meaningful...or perhaps not.

That day when I went to the clinic, Harry came.

'Hello Natasha. May I come in?'

'Of course. You don't need to ask.'

'Okay. I've ordered coffee. I hope you have some time?'

'Yes, Harry, I always have time for you. Tell me, anything special?'

'What are you now...a die...?'

'Dietician. It is my job to tell the patients what food will be suitable for them based on their disease.'

'Oh, so tell me too.'

'Sure. You're gaining weight. You need to be very careful. You must take a walk every morning, Harry.'

'Oh no. I'm scared of the breeze ghost, Natasha!'

'Come on, don't be silly. There is no ghost in the breeze, Harry. It's clean and pure.'

'No, ghosts do exist. When Sister Dorothy and Elena... Dheera...when they go for a walk, the ghost catches hold of them. God knows how they behave. It makes me fearful.'

The coffee arrived. I breathed a sigh of relief. Oh dear, what had this poor, innocent boy seen?

'Come, let's have coffee and you can tell me how the

other patients are doing.'

'Okay, Natasha.'

One of my patients arrived just then. Harry wanted to leave, but I said, 'Stay here, Harry. It's okay.' He stood against the wall.

The woman put her file on the desk. She looked quite melancholy. She also seemed to be pregnant. She sat down on the chair where Harry had been sitting.

I opened the file and read it. 'I am sorry, Vinita ji, but your report doesn't look too good. It indicates that the child is not normal.'

Harry dropped his cup of coffee. The liquid splattered on the floor. He quickly brought a towel from the bathroom and wiped the floor with it. He also wiped the stains from Vinita's saree slowly.

Vinita said impatiently, 'Tell me, Doctor, what does my report say? What's wrong?'

'It shows your child isn't normal. He may be born with Down's Syndrome.' Just getting these words out shook my soul. I looked from Harry to the report and back. Vinita's face was white.

'Can you help me?' she said. 'Can some diet help? Any medicine?'

I looked at her in surprise. In my brief experience as a dietician, this was the first such case.

'I don't think, Vinita ji, there is any food item or herb

that could work a miracle. At least as a dietician I am not aware of any. I can only suggest a diet for you and the child, if you wish.'

'That's fine, but if the child is not normal what's the use? Please suggest... should I abort? Destroy it? It was my dream to have a baby, but now I don't know what to do.'

Her eyes filled with tears.

'No, madam, no! Don't do that. Please....'Harry shouted and ran out of the room. 'No! No!'

His voice rang in the hospital corridor, putting both Vinita and me in a dilemma. We both sat around in silence for a while. Then she picked up her file quietly and left. I don't know what she thought, but sometimes in adverse circumstances something auspicious does happen. A fragrant yellow rose is born on a bush full of thorns.

Mandira and I sat opposite each other. Despite the refreshing scent of the coffee neither of us could have it.

'Do you want something else, ma'am?' the waiter asked, putting the plate of sandwiches before us.

'No, thanks.'

'Come, have some. How long will you sit like this?' Mandira helped herself to a sandwich, so I had to take one too.

'Tell me something, Natasha ... you allowed Papaji to go and what kind of life are you living here alone in this dingy little room? You never told anyone that your thesis has been accepted by the University of Yale. They want to publish it and introduce it in their curriculum. If you wanted, you could also have gone. For so many years you not only studied Psychology, but lived it. When you are there your life will take a new turn and you will make progress.'

'Come, finish your coffee. It'll go cold.'

'You're the one who's gone cold. It seems there's no life left in you. How long will you live like a hermit?'

'Mandira, there's nothing like that. I feel it was the right time for Papaji to go. Had he stayed back he would have had a nervous breakdown. What did he get all his life? He went on making sacrifices for everyone—sacrificed himself, his wishes and desires—sometimes for his wife, sometimes for his son. He could never attain the kind of home and family happiness he had dreamt of. And in that desire he forgot himself. And then I entered his life...and began to haunt him as a symbol of his defeat. He might have recovered from Shailendra's loss, but he began to run from me. He avoided me. He would leave home early in the morning and return late at night. What could be a better escape or plan for him than to go abroad? And that too at such a respectable position where his intellectual ability will be appreciated—something every intelligent person wants in life.'

'Maybe you're right, Natasha. Since I'm your friend I worry about your future. I'm not concerned about anyone else.'

'Thanks, Mandira. Your support is not only needed, but is very important to me.'

Another cup of coffee arrived.

'Mandira, I spoke to them. Sir Rajnarayan's brother stays in Edinburgh. He will look after Papaji... I am happy for him.'

'But you're mad, Natasha. You're sacrificing your dreams and happiness for him. What kind of dream are you living?'

'I'm a psychologist. I spend my time here teaching people how to dream. I pull them out of depression, fear, lack of motivation, etc. and show them how to live with self-respect.'

'But now you're a dietician, madam.'

'Yes, I am, but even for that I first need to understand human emotions. Food habits come later. Oh, I wanted to tell you. A few months ago a young man came to this hospital. He was admitted here. He's a writer and the disaster was that he lost three fingers of his right hand in some accident. In fact, he was lucky to have survived, but the pain of the experience compounded with the loss of his fingers was too much for him to take. But Mandira, it was amazing that he never complained. I remember he said to Dr Sandeep one day, "Doctor, it's very difficult for me to deal with my family and so called friends who say all kinds of things regarding my injury. They equate it to bizarre things. When I analyze their barbed comments I see no sympathy, mercy or love. It's more of a disguised rebellion, an insult or smugness that I will never be able to write again."

'Dr Sandeep spoke encouragingly to him as he used to to me. "You are wise my dear friend. Thank God that you managed to live after seeing death at such close quarters. You must understand that strength comes from the depth of your heart, and from the earth, through your legs, into your chest, into your heart, not from the arm or fingers. That strength will help you write again."

'And Mandira, he closed his eyes and mumbled a prayer I think.'

Vidyawati ji was leaving. It was the day she visited the railway platform. To remember a stranger's death and pay a tribute every month affected me quite a lot. How many people in the world actually remember others who have been kind to them during difficult times? And then Papaji wants me to forget Shailendra and marry again. Had he been able to forget Kamini ji?

'I'm going, beta. I've cooked lunch. Have it whenever you feel like it. I'll come back soon. It's Navratri today. I've to do my puja also.'

'Alright. Thanks to your puja this house remains so sacred and clean, Vidyawati ji. After Papaji left you've been my only anchor. I really owe you a lot. You maintain this house as a home.'

I stood up and hugged her. She patted my head affectionately.

'Bhai ji left me responsible for you. And then you're so young. You're so absorbed in your work and your studies that if I don't cook you would just lie around neither eating nor complaining. Okay, I'll leave now—the rickshaw-wala has come.'

How I wish we could have made a memorial for Shailendra. Everything was lapped up by the flames in the pyre. His body, his essence was erased. What if his body had been preserved in a coffin? I would have gone and paid him homage on his birthday. I would have had an opportunity to kneel in front of it for the sake of our love.

But for our rules and regulations that say the body must be burnt and returned to the five elements—air, water, fire, earth and aether (space). Shailendra's body—the beautiful body was reduced to ashes. Only a picture of him on the wall remained—a smiling shadow, pure and peaceful.

Now when I came to the clinic and sat down on my dietician's chair I felt somewhat anxious. Perhaps because my research was related to Psychology. On the one hand I found distinctive equations in emotions; on the other, the distinct relationship between food and physical problems. On that chair I felt I was sitting under a tree where old leaves fell dead every day, new leaves were born and new buds blossomed.

These days young women come to me quite often, especially the ones who want to lose weight to look slim like film stars. I feel good preparing food charts for them based on their blood group. I enjoy seeing new confidence and motivation on their faces. It carries me from simple selfishness (my fees) to total selflessness. A self-created journey of the soul.

The door opened and the sound of voices brought me back to the present.

'Arrey beta, how are you, Natasha?'

'Oh, it's you, Zubaida ji.' I stood up.

'Behen ji...' Sahil was in a clean white kurta pyjama saying *Khuda Hafiz* to someone.

'Oh Sahil, you look good.' I touched him lightly. Right then a young woman in a deep red sharara and kurta, a pretty little flower, came and stood next to him.

'Arrey, I've been looking for you for so long, beta. Then Sister Dorothy told me....And Dr Prashant too mentioned the injustice you've suffered. This is destiny...your husband?' She put her hand on my head.

'Please sit down, Zubaida ji. Sahil's looking great.'

She wiped her eyes with her dupatta and said, 'Thanks to your prayers and the treatment here my Sahil has recovered. There's such a spiritual quality to you too, beta. How do you manage your life...and now your patients?'

'I don't know. Anyway, you tell me....'

'I got Sahil married. Now everything is fine. This is his new bride.' She prodded the hesitant girl towards me.

'Oh, congratulations. Such a lovely bride you have, Sahil. I hope you're happy now. You should start life anew.'

Sahil had not spoken a word so far. Nor did his face show any expression. He stayed silent. Zubaida ji pushed a box of sweets towards me and said, 'Here, have some.'

'Let's go, Ammi.' He turned around and left. Zubaida ji took the new bride's hand in hers and said to me, 'Okay beta, *khuda hafiz.* Let me give you some advice. You too should marry. God willing, your life will light up again. How young you are! It will be difficult to live all alone. Life is a long journey. Think about it.'

The door opened and Sahil walked in again. 'Ammi, let's go. Stop giving unsolicited advice. You talk too much.' He took her hand and dragged her away. The perplexed bride followed anxiously. The box of sweets lay quietly on my desk. Some words stuck to me and my situation like ghosts.

Sundays used to be free, especially after Papaji left. So I started spending them with Amma and Baba.

This time when I reached home I saw Baba lying on the bed with his eyes closed. His body looked weak. When I touched him I realized he had high fever. Amma was in the kitchen.

'Oh, when did you come?' She stood holding a glass of black solution in her hand. 'And how long have you been sitting here holding Baba's hand and weeping?'

'I just came in, Amma.' I leapt to my feet and embraced her. The contact with her body made me even more anxious. 'You never told me—how long has he been sick? Tomorrow I'll take him to the hospital and get all the tests done.'

'Come, sit. What could I have told you? You have your own problems. You work all day and study at night.'

She handed the glass to Baba, who started sipping it slowly. 'Has your course finished, beta?'

'Yes, Baba. Now I run a clinic. Besides the hospital, some patients come to me at the clinic too. But forget all that. Tell me, what medicine is this? Which doctor did you consult?'

'Beta, you already know I never go to doctors. It's only vaidya ji—Dr Ram Sharan Mishra—the one who treated you and Urvashi when you were children.'

'Baba, you too? The world has changed so much and you're still taking the local, bitter *kaadha*.'

'Yes, beta. I trust him the most. You remember there was

a tumour in my stomach? Doctors used to say it would have to be operated, but thanks to Mishra ji's herbs it dissolved on its own. I wanted him to treat Shailendra too, but never said a word fearing the doctors. And then everybody there thought us to be illiterate fools.'

'Arrey Baba, it wasn't like that. Shailendra didn't have a disease; he lost his faculties in an accident.'

Amma took back the empty glass from Baba. 'Beta, we go on living, but Shailendra's loss has shaken us up badly. We worry about you a lot.'

Then tears again. Hiding them Amma retreated into the kitchen. Baba and I stayed back. A knock on the door pulled us out of our thoughts.

It was vaidyaji. His face was neat, impressive and strangely radiant with a broad forehead marked with sandalwood paste. He wore a white dhoti kurta. He entered smelling of incense. 'Arrey bhai, Chaman Lal, how are you? Has the fever come down or not?'

I got up and offered him a chair. I touched his feet. He kept his hand on my head and blessed me...*Ayushman bhava*

'Oh it's you Natasha beti. How are you? How's your health?'

'I am fine, thank you.'

'Chaman Lal told me ... but this is Destiny. It cannot be erased.'

'True....'I could no longer shed tears or utter a word.

Vaidya ji checked Baba's pulse with his eyes closed. In the silence the maid brought a glass of water for him and left it on the stool. He let go of Baba's wrist and checked his eyes. Then he examined his stomach.

'Chaman bhai, you seem better. Just have *kaadha* for another two days. Your tumour is absolutely fine now. Still, get an X–Ray done to make sure.'

Amma brought some *mathris* made of ghee on a plate and two glasses of *thandai*.

'Arrey, Behen ji, why did you bother....? But you do remember that I love your *mathris*.' And he picked up a *mathri* and put it in his mouth.

'Okay...tell me beta, what are you doing these days?'He looked towards me.

'I work at a hospital as a food specialist for the patients. I look after their diet. I have completed a course in it—a special course. I am a dietitian.'

'Oh, so there are food specialists these days?'

'Yes, vaidya ji. For different diseases one needs different regimes. What can harm the person in his or her condition? Or what kind of diet should a pregnant woman have?'

'Oh I see. We could tell people that much ourselves. We never had specialists for that earlier.' He had had two *mathris* by then. Suddenly, I remembered Vinita. 'Vaidya ji, may I ask you something?'

'Yes, beta. Go ahead.'

'I have a patient. She is pregnant. Her reports show that her child is not mentally developed fully. She is very worried. She cannot decide whether she should keep the child or abort it. I've been trying to do some research for her, but haven't found any reliable treatment.'

'Beta, there are certainly some treatments which work better than herbs, I can tell you.'

'Really?' I stared at him in amazement.

'Do something. Tell her to have milk in a silver tumbler first thing in the morning. After that she should put a hand on her womb and read out a mantra—once in the morning looking towards the sun. Once in the afternoon. And once in the evening before the sun sets.'

'Mantra! What use is a mantra, vaidya ji? These are internal physical defects.' I was hesitant.

'*Bin nainan sab jag dekhe—lochan achte andha. Kehet Kabir kuch samjhipari hai, yeh jag dekhya andha*. Beta, what the eyes see is not always the truth. It is only a dream. What you can see is a view, but don't believe it. Using your eyes you cannot even see yourself. Then how can you see the reality? How can someone who doesn't have self-knowledge have the ultimate knowledge? I don't know about your medicine and treatments. I diagnose diseases with my inner knowledge and treat them the same way. If you wish to believe in it I can give you the mantra.'

'If you don't take it otherwise, vaidya ji, may I ask how

a mantra can cure a physical defect?'

'I don't know how deep the knowledge of your generation is. In our times, in education, the mind and soul were considered of primary importance. Not only this, but in Chemistry too drugs were woven into plain tales of righteousness and religion. Our education was linked with devotion to God.'

After sometime he said, 'Our shastras consider the "word" as the creator of the world. A word is a wave of consciousness. Their correct pronunciation and the echo of their sound—special and pervasive—is considered a manifestation of God. This expression connects us to Godliness. And you may find it surprising, beta, but I'd like to tell you that not just man but entire natural processes are linked to this word.'

'Oh, I never thought of that. Where can we find its evidence?'

'Where will you look for it? In the Vedas it has been presented in the form of '*anhad-naad*' or *akashvani* ('pri modal sound' or 'voice from heaven'). In the *Upanishads* the 'word' has been called '*udgeet*'. And Sufi saints call it *'saufe-sarmad'* (everlasting mysticism).'

I was lost in the wave of a unique, unparalleled experience. There was so much to learn in the world. And here we mistakenly celebrated our successes and achievements, making a mountain out of a grain.

'So may I leave now, Chaman Lal? Just have your *kaadha*.'

'And meals? Should I give him *khichdi* or yellow dal with roti?'

'Anything. Whatever he wants to have. You can also try a *mathri*; it's very tasty.' As he stood up to leave Amma said, 'Wait, I'll pack some *mathris* for you. You can take them home.' She disappeared inside.

'Vaidya ji, please could you give me that mantra? Let me try it on my patient and see the miraculous effects of your *'anhad-naad'* or 'word' or whatever.'

'Alright. Let me give it to you. Treating the sick and social work is my duty anyway.'

And he wrote down the mantra for me on a piece of paper. Taking the packet of *mathris* from Amma with a smile, he left humming a tune to himself.

I remembered that ever since I had completed the dietician's course I had neither enjoyed the mathris, nor the samosas from *Simran*. And vaidyaji? He had had *mathris* fried in real ghee made by Amma herself. Could this really be a form of treatment? Was it just friendship or detachment?

Vinita came when I phoned her. I looked at her entire file. There were hazy images of her child in the reports. According to Dr Prashant's reports the child was not mentally normal, but the pregnancy was now five months old and the foetus could not be aborted.

'Now Natasha, you tell me what to do.'

'Vinita ji, you cannot abort the child. You will have to keep him or her, and give birth. I've researched your case well. I've also found some medication. I'll write it down for you. Take it morning and evening. And yes...there is a vaidya ji we know. I spoke to him about your case. I'll also explain whatever he said. It's not difficult. I guess you can have milk in a silver tumbler....'

'Why only silver?'

'Every element has chemical properties, Vinita. Copper has some; bell metal has its own, but maybe glass does not have any. How does it matter? If you don't have a glass you could use a bowl or something...but silver.'

'Okay, I'll buy one.'

'Yes. Apart from that there is a mantra.' I handed the handwritten mantra to her. 'You have to read it out three times a day—at sunrise, midday and sunset, with your hand on your womb, with hope.'

'Oh, how will that help?' she gawked at me.

'It will influence the child's health. You must have heard about Abhimanyu's story in the *Mahabharata*. When he was still in his mother's womb, before he was born, he had already learnt how to break into a *chakravyuh*—a trap created to kill him.'

'Oh yes I remember. I saw it in a television serial. But it was quite unbelievable.'

'But it was true. History is witness that it happened.'

'Oh really?' She thought for a while. 'But maybe you didn't pay attention, Natasha ji, I'm not a Hindu but a Christian. How will I chant a mantra?'

'Oh, I didn't realize....'I looked at the name on her file. Vinita Mathhew.

It was a strange paradox. Both of us fell silent, searching for something within ourselves.

'Listen Vinita, no matter what the name...the human body is the same. You and I have similar bodies, don't we? This ancient mantra is just written in Sanskrit for the living, breathing child in your womb. It doesn't care what the name is—Hindu or Christian. Don't bring religion into this. Try it for the sake of your baby. It's not difficult. Consider it a magic charm.'

'Natasha, being a doctor you're speaking of magic charms and mantra chanting? Strange.'

'Vinita, I don't believe in them myself, but vaidya ji has challenged me. Let's see.'

Forget Sanskrit, Vinita did not even know Hindi properly. I wrote the mantra for her in Roman Hindi. Maybe another experiment....

I remembered during the viva my examiner had asked me to define generativity. In a moment of generativity, flowing with our emotions, we choose that point of view that is good for us or gives us pleasure or the point of view that provides our consciousness the state of mind which helps us deal with worldly sorrows. And the interesting thing is that slowly this generativity becomes a mental process that brings about change and introduces us to our own inner desires and areas of interest. With such a mindset, man can experience a new desire and attain new horizons.

Arrey, I thought, I had been progressing in this direction step by step. Then how did the explosion happen suddenly?

Where had I arrived walking along that my horizon itself had disappeared? What skies had I wandered under? In so many years in the hospital, all the mistakes and foolishness, all ties, all hopes, dreams for the future had broken. After Shailendra's death there was a strange nothingness, an absolute silence in which I was drowning. Somehow, I had to save myself.

The hospital had become my future, but the route had changed. I took the lift to the second floor straight to my dietician's clinic, which was a bit different. Instead of Psychology my iPad now has my patients' reports, blood groups and diet charts. Mostly they are young men and women suffering from obesity, who want to lose weight to look good. Harry comes daily. He makes me laugh. He has coffee with me.

The other day I had gathered my papers and was preparing to leave when Sister Dorothy came in. The door shut on its own after her.

'How are you, Natasha?'

'Sister, I'm good. And you?'

'I miss you, maybe also because the bench you sat on for so many months now lies empty most of the time. Anyway, you never come that side?'

'How can I, Sister?'

'Yes, I know.' Then she came and stood very close to me. 'Natasha, you've become quite lonely, haven't you? I'd like to help you overcome that loneliness. It's very difficult to live alone. I want to redefine pleasure for you—safe sex.' She said so much without hesitation.

'Please, Sister....'I was in a state of strange confusion.

'No, Natasha! Come and see. Tomorrow is Saturday. Come over and we'll have tea together. I'll wait for you in my cottage, okay?'

She took my hands in hers. Her eyes had a strange expression as though trying to communicate something. I trembled. 'Try, Natasha. Sex is a need. The body needs it just as it needs food and water. The ones who don't accept it are hypocrites. They fear the society. But we don't.'

'Please, Sister. I have a lot of respect for you, but I

won't be able to come.'

'Think about it, Natasha. I'll wait.' She turned around and left. I sat down on a chair heavily. What kind of an experience was this? I had learnt to form character through knowledge and devotion. And my love, my sense of gratification had deepened towards the emptiness Shailendra had left behind. I was trying to turn my passion towards my work. The life lived with Shailendra, his memories are my prayer and reason for living. The pleasurable moments shared with him are enough for life.

Sister Dorothy informed me that Vinita had given birth to a baby boy. Harry came running after her. Still panting he put a yellow rose on my desk.

'Thanks, Natasha.'

'Thanks for what, Harry?'

'Because upon your insistence she did not abort the child.'

'Oh, but I'm a bit nervous. Sister, what if the child isn't normal? Her family will kill me.'

'Come and see her,' said Harry.

'No, not yet. After Dr Chapekar's report comes in.'

They left. The rose lying on my desk glared at me. I had assured Vinita all would be well...and given her medicines.

And Vaidya ji's mantra? I felt I was walking on a tightrope with medicines in one hand and vaidya ji's mantra in the other, trying to balance myself—with danger and risk on either side. My balance wasn't too firm.

I lived with my anxiety for two days, still walking the tightrope, but trying to hold on to my faith. I had never faced such a dilemma before. Dr Chapekar's phone call filled me with great dread. He had called me to the hospital lounge. I reached there partly with fear and partly with regret.

In the lounge along with Dr Chapekar stood Vinita's husband. The moment he saw me the doctor reached out and hugged me. Strange. Dr Prashant was always so reserved, so grave, I thought. Vinita's husband too came forward and took my hand. 'Thank you, Natasha ji. I have no words. My child is absolutely normal. I will never forget your kindness.' He kissed my hand.

'Oh...I am so happy. Doctor, are you sure he is normal?'

'Yes, Natasha, yes. This is the result of your medical and emotional support.'

I ran into Vinita's room. 'Congratulations, Vinita.'

I picked up the infant. He had a round, pretty face, pointed nose, broad forehead and surprisingly thick hair. Such a beautiful child. Like a delicate flower. Vinita was crying. 'Natasha ji, I will never forget your compassion and gentleness.' She held my hands tightly.

'Thank God. All is well when it ends well. I am happy

too, Vinita, that the child is normal.'

'Natasha ji, I took the medicines you gave me regularly and followed all the instructions you had given, including chanting that mantra three times a day.' Then she whispered, 'I liked the ritual. Then, Natasha, to tell you the truth my grandfather was a Hindu. At a little distance from here is the city of Hathras. He was a school teacher there. When my father started working for the railways he changed his faith. Otherwise, we would have still been Hindus and practiced the same rites.'

'Oh, that's good. Now take good care of the child.'

I came out. In the corridor next to the lounge was the wall with the carvings of the various gods. Along with Jesus hanging on the cross was the carving of Krishna playing his flute. For the first time I felt like bowing before the Gods I had never believed in, with complete devotion.

Upon returning from the clinic I called Baba. 'Baba, this is Natasha. I need something from you. Please give me the phone number and address of vaidya ji—I want to go and meet him right now.'

'Why, what happened? Are you alright?'

'Yes, I'm fine. Absolutely fine. But I need to see him.'

'But beta, Mishra ji left for Varanasi two months ago. He said he wouldn't be coming back. He has renounced the world and has taken *sanyas*.'

'Oh.' I slumped upon a chair. I opened the drawer and

rummaged through it. The piece of paper with the mantra lay there intact.

The next day when I reached Vinita's room Dr Chapekar was already there examining the baby. When he saw me he said, 'Natasha, I believe you gave Mrs Matthew some medicine? Because I'm quite confused about how this child could be absolutely normal. I compared both her reports, the old one and the new one. I'm amazed. Last time the symptoms were very different; Down's Syndrome was very clear. And now? I checked the child again. Strange. This is the first time I've seen something like this. Tell me, Mrs Matthew, what was the name of the medicine you took?'

'Okay, Doctor.' She pulled out the piece of paper with the name of the medicine from her file and handed it to him. 'This is it, but Doctor, there was another medicine—faith. Do you have faith in God?'

'Oh, what are you saying? Faith in God confuses me even more, though I believe in God. It opens up another path. I don't know about Christianity, but in our medical studies we rely on chemical processes the most, not on faith in God.'

'Even I never believed in God, Dr Prashant, because I too felt that faith in God could only open a can of worms. But then I thought I would experiment once. And then I discovered that belief invariably removed a lot of confusion from life.'

'Doctor, I never believed in any religion or God. But

I believed in an unseen power, in a sound, in some words I didn't even know how to pronounce properly. Nor did I know what they meant. Upon Natasha's insistence I just believed in that mantra. It could be faith...or God.'

'Amazing. So then ... isn't faith related to the intellect? Is it not practical?'

'I really don't know.'

It's been more than two years since Shailendra went away. I still can't bring myself to say 'since he died'. And about a year since Papaji's left. I have learnt to live alone.

That day, having bought a new car, I was returning home—a home, where nobody waited for me. Vidyawatiji sat under the tree on the platform. She was thrilled to see me step out of the car.

'Arrey beta, you've bought a new car? Congratulations.'

'Yes, Vidywati ji. Thanks to your blessings I earn well now. Come, let me take you for a drive.'

'Oh...why me? I...'She hesitated. 'It's a new car, beta. Take your parents for a ride, not me.'

'Why? Do you mean less to me than my parents? Like an elder of the house you take care of everything with so much love and commitment. You were with Papaji and me through all our trials and tribulations. Even now you're with me like the comforting shade of a tree.' I hugged her with tears in my eyes.

She patted my head affectionately and said, 'It's thanks to Bhaiji and you that I'm living a respectable life. Otherwise I was rotting in hell—oh what trials I suffered! Had Bhaiji not brought me here as his sister I would have wasted away amongst the old, diseased, lifeless people at the Home—just like he was spending his days alone swallowing his tears. I would have perished in some dark, secluded corner. The afflictions of age are like that—they leave you at a juncture where you simply turn into stone. And no children want to understand that pain. Isn't that surprising?'

'But you showed a great deal of courage after a life of such torment...You didn't lose hope. You started a new life—learnt to read and write. I really liked that. Actually, what happens is—when life falls off-track and you begin to feel that nothing's left in it, that there is no hope or happiness left, it takes a new turn. A new chapter begins...a new journey. And that gives you direction.'

'Then you should also move ahead, Natasha. Have you thought about a new life?'

'Arrey Vidyawati ji...I'm doing so much, see. I'm a dietician now. A lot of young women come to me to help them lose weight. My medication helps them. I'm famous amongst the new generation modern women. That's why I could buy this car. Otherwise, how could I have accomplished this?'

'That's alright...I'm happy that you're doing well. You read and write so much and I'm glad to see that. But let me repeat what Bhaiji said, beta. He wanted you to remarry. You're still very young. Life is long. It's very tough to live alone. Tell me... during all this time haven't you found anybody you like? Any doctor or friend?' She laughed.

'No Vidyawati ji. Until now, I have not felt any such desire. Every time Papaji calls he repeats the same thing. He said he would return when I had some good news to give him. What kind of a condition is this? The house has become so silent since he left. I'm going to write a letter to him tonight. Maybe he'll come back when he reads it.'

'Alright. Do that. Come, let's go and meet your Amma. Let her see your new car.'

'Amma and Baba have gone to visit Urvashi in Kanpur. Her date of delivery is close. Amma couldn't travel alone, so Baba had to accompany her. It will be a nice change for them. They never left Agra after Shailendra's death or they could have taken a pilgrimage or something.'

'Oh I see.'

'Once Urvashi's child is born I'll visit her in Kanpur. Why don't you come with me? When she got married Shailendra and I were in Singapore—I never even met her husband. I had my own troubles to deal with; what could I do?'

'Okay. We'll certainly go and wish her, but first you must think about your own future. You're getting older every year.'

'Age. Why, I never thought about it.'

As usual, before going to bed I started checking my emails on my iPad. The ones related to my work were separate, but Papaji's mails were making me restless. Most of them contained general news about his friends' families or the weather, the beauty of the snowfall or ill health because of the cold. Through each of them he wanted to convey the sadness of living a solitary life. So I shut down my iPad. Are these letters on the machine even letters? Straight and lacking in sympathy.

I took out a floral piece of paper from my drawer and began to write on it.

Dear Papaji,

I have been receiving all your emails, but they don't have the beauty of your handwriting. Nor do the words carry the meaning that penetrates into the heart. Something or the other is always missed out, especially the warmth of affection that I really need. Papaji, it'll be nice if you write letters once in a while. At least I'll have a document to treasure and that will spread the fragrance of your love in this house.

Today I'm going to answer the question that has been of utmost concern to you. Papaji, you want me to marry again and settle down in life. Let me assure you I'm quite settled, at peace with my inner self and settled in my profession. You know that with time I have also carved a niche for myself as a dietician, which gives me enough fulfilment. This is my nourishment.

When I think of marriage, of sharing my life with someone, no one around me fits into that image. The thread that bound me to Shailendra is unbreakable. Papaji, I'm sure you must have felt the same way when kamini ji left you. You lived a private life, like a sanyasi. I admire your humanity. My soul is touched by your simplicity. You are my pillar of strength and my guide. If you could sail through this ocean of life with all its adversities, I should also be able to do so.

What a coincidence. Someone just sent me a beautiful story on my mobile. I'm quoting it here:

> He left her in the middle of the night—the night her son was born. When she heard the news she was devastated. Yet she did not complain. She decided to live for her son. She wanted him to grow up to be a man the world would look up to.
>
> Her relatives and friends came and asked her to forget the man who had left over and begin anew. They asked her to remarry, but she refused. She was young

and beautiful. Suitors queued up outside her door, but she refused each one of them.

Then one day he came back...her husband. He stood in front of her. She could hardly remember him as the man who had left her.

'They call you Buddha now?' she asked him gently.

'I hear they do,' he answered calmly.

'What does it mean?'

'I think it means The Enlightened One.'

She smiled. There was silence.

'I suppose we have both learnt something. You've learnt, O Buddha, to make the world richer in spirit, but my lesson ... my lesson, unfortunately, will remain largely unknown.'

'And what lesson is that?' he enquired.

Her eyes sparkled; the tears remained unshed. 'That a courageous woman does not need anyone to complete her. She is complete on her own.'

Can't the spirit of Yashodhara be my answer too, Papaji?

With warm regards...

Natasha

An invitation card fluttered on my desk. Mandira had called already. 'Natasha, you're coming this evening, aren't you? Rajiv, my cousin Rajiv, has built a new house. Hence the party. Be there on time. I'll be there with Zafar.'

'Alright, I'll try.'

'No, don't try. You have to come. No excuses, okay.'

A lot of new houses had come up beyond Hari Parvat. The driver stopped the car outside one of them, which looked quite pretty. Hesitantly, I made my way inside. I had no idea what the people would be like. I knew nobody except Mandira. A modern looking woman welcomed me at the door.

'Hi, I'm Vandana, Rajiv Chandra's wife. And you are...?'

'Natasha Mehra. I'm Mandira's friend.' I shook her hand.

'Oh...welcome. Yes, you are the famous dietician. I've heard of you. Please come in.'

'Thanks.' I followed her into a large hall where several other people were gathered. Mandira emerged from the crowd and greeted me.

'Natasha, you're here! Well done, Rajiv...this is my friend, Natasha. She's a dietician at City Hospital.'

'Oh hello. I'm Avantika. Do you recognize me? Your client—Avantika Raje?'

'Yes, I do. How are you?'

Vandana stepped forward and took my hand. 'Come,

let me introduce you to other people too.' Her touch was gentle; she had a pleasant face and a special, unique voice quality. I was not accustomed to it. The other women also seemed to belong to the modern new society. Drinks in their hands and in their eyes...? I didn't know what...what kind of an inviting expression. There was a bar close by. A couple of women stood next to it. I noticed—was that Pooja's mother? Yes, it was her. I headed in her direction. I wanted to ask her how Pooja was. But the minute she recognized me she turned and vanished to the other end of the room.

'That lady is Mrs Awasthi,' said Vandana. 'The wife of the biggest industrialist here.'

Just then Rajiv asked, 'What will you have?'

'I don't know.' I had left behind my acquaintance with drinks in Singapore.

'Come Natasha, try this—it's sherry.'

'Oh, it's you, sir.' Dr Sandeep stood with Rajiv.

'Yes, Natasha. Do you know how sherry is described? It's rich and bloody.' He handed me a glass with a smile. I liked its colour and the description was interesting. The glass itself was artistic. So I had to have the drink.

'Cheers,' said Dr Sandeep and Rajiv, clinking their glasses against mine. Mandira had arrived by then. She too joined us and said, 'Cheers.'

'Vandana ji, your house is very tastefully done. What

do you do? Interiors or...?'

'Oh no no ... Vandana Bhabhi is only a housewife,' replied Mandira.

'No, Mandira ji, I'm going for Vedanta classes these days,' said Vandana. Her mannerisms were quite western.

'Very interesting. You're doing quite well. Tell me something about Vedanta. I did Psychology, then Science... became a dietician, a food specialist...and have moved far away from spirituality and knowledge of the soul.'

'It's fashionable to talk about spirituality these days. Another new craze is Buddhist chanting.' In Vandana's hand was a glass of whisky and irony shone in her eyes. 'Natasha ji, people these days socialize more in the name of religion. It's the lifestyle of the modern society.'

'Oh dear, here you are, Mandira! I missed you. And I remember...you're Natasha, Mandira's closest friend.' Zafar wrapped me in his arms and hugged me. I shivered. Then pulling back he said, 'Come Natasha, let me introduce you to a friend. He's a very good writer.'

We walked ahead. Some people were sitting on chairs looking grave. I overheard someone talking.

'It's very difficult to emerge from a blow like that. I don't wish to complain. And who can I complain to anyway? Or to thank someone hesitantly—or be obliged to thank someone. Who? God...or the doctor who saved my life, but couldn't save my hand?'

I turned around. Yes, I had seen him on television and in our hospital. It was shown as a major accident. I remembered—maybe it was a case of a parcel bomb. His life was saved after the blast, but the fingers of his right hand and part of the palm were cut off. Hurt, unrecognizable, emboldened right hand—it now lay in a black leather glove.

When the incident occurred, it was discovered that the conspiracy had been hatched by some close friend or family member, not an enemy. The television repeats the same piece of news so many times that the image gets stuck in your mind even if you don't want it.

'Still, Mihir,' said Zafar. 'You're very brave. In spite of such a big loss you've attained success. The book you launched last month has been getting good reviews. People have praised it. I read your scientific analysis, in which you have raised significant questions about the deliberations of the human mind. It is pretty complex. Difficult to understand. Our intellectual society focuses on the energy in man and contemplation on it, but you hold the mind itself responsible for these workings.'

'But Rajiv, these computers interfering with man's mental explorations have overshadowed his capabilities and energy. Next, this machine...intelligence, will also start thinking like humans.'

'Then what about those memories and experiences so personal to man or which are preserved in his creative mind?

Somewhere deep down in his heart?'

Mihir turned to me. His eyes were like lightning. 'You are right,' he said. 'Times are such that the effects of computers and their constant progress have filled us with rage, because computers have become supra conceptual, bridging huge distances and occupying mental space. Nobody needs to think anymore.'

'Yes, you speak the truth. Now we don't need to work for intelligence as we had to earlier. Remember, Mandira—how we used to recite tables? 8 x 4 = 32...or count the names of the Mughal rulers on our fingers? And then the commentaries in Sanskrit and grammar? Now if you want to know anything you don't need to look within. Just open your iPad and you'll find everything written on its miniature screen instantly, without putting any pressure on your mind.' Mandira was standing next to me.

'Earlier the encyclopedia used to be our legacy. I remember how my mother would save money to buy these books for us. They're still a precious bequest for me, but aren't they losing their identity?'

'But now you don't need to buy books at all. No matter what you want to read, just go to Amazon. Literature, new or old, anything at all will be in front of you in a matter of seconds.'

'But yaar there was a romance associated with the physical touch of books. The sound of the turning pages made one's heart race. During university days as people dropped and picked up books and their fingers touched, it had its own charm. Do you remember the movie *Mere Mehboob*?'

Lost in some memories Zafar sat holding Mandira's hand.

'Now computers are writing new literature. God knows how it will be. Mechanical? Enchanting? Or devoid of emotion, which will be unable to move anybody?' Mihir looked at me. 'So what will it be like?'

'Machines cannot be human. Their intelligence draws a frail, but sharp line between physical and intellectual capacity of man.'

'Yes. One will have to think about it.' His hands shook. He drank the entire whisky in his glass in one gulp.

'So will machines override all of man's gentler emotions and memories? What about the emotions that cast lifelong impact on the human heart? What about them? Will machines ever be able to express a fraction of them?'

'Nothing will happen. In any case what is the value of human emotions today? Nothing at all.'

'Then what's the point of living? Why do we think our identity has some meaning? Why are we alive at all?' Mihir's face looked sad. In fact all of us felt somewhat depressed.

'Well, if we are here to test the sense of belonging and identity today, why shouldn't we make our own lives influential?'

'You're talking about existence; I've been living this

tough phase of my life wandering amongst ruins. I could feel some substance, some life in them. When I slept at night I would feel some part of the life gone by stand next to me and whisper something in my ear...some mystery.'

'You're lucky you could sleep. I try all night that some divine intervention, some divine dream would exert itself upon my existence so that I can sleep, but I cannot. What your Vedantas describe as deep sleep, Avantika ji,' he said, looking at her.

'You need to meditate for that.'

'We're speaking of the era of machines. We doctors only believe in a scientific point of view.' Dr Sandeep had brought another glass of whisky for Mihir.

'Yes, Doctor. Today the human mind has become more interesting because of the progress of machines. It heralds greater challenges in the times to come.'

I couldn't resist saying, 'No, Mihir ji. No matter how machine-like the scientists become we psychologists can never dissociate our emotions from our mind—what you call spirituality or religious consciousness.'

Mihir gave me a strange glance.

'If you separate them...life, thought, soul...all will become mud.'

'And mud has no religion.'

'It is neither man nor machine.'

He had come over to stand right next to me. He put

his gloved hand on my shoulder.

'Oh.' I shivered all over, but oblivious to it his unwelcome hand stayed where it was.

'I don't know who you are or what you do, but you can argue well.'

He turned around and his gaze settled on my face. The darkness of his eyes was disconcerting, but his sharp, three-dimensional look was tenacious enough to leave its imprint upon me. Something pricked my insides. Like a big thorn. I didn't know what it was. The coldness of the glance made me lose my balance. My hands trembled and I dropped the glass of sherry I had been holding. It shattered on the floor. The blood-red liquid scattered on the white marble floor in the middle of the conversation.

'Sorry. I'm very sorry.' Embarrassed, I stood like a statue, trying to steer the folds of my saree away from the mess.

'Don't worry, Natasha.'

'This is also an element of human intellect.' Rajiv tried to salvage the situation.

'But what a paradox. Machines or computers can do whatever they like, but they cannot shed blood, Dr Sandeep.'

I bent down to stop the flow of the sherry—rich and bloody—that was staining the spotless white floor with its colour. My handkerchief alone was not enough to restrict the flow.

'Don't. Don't wipe it, Natasha...the waiter's coming.'

Rajiv pulled me back up. Close to me I heard a rustle of silk and the laughter of Pooja's mother. I had heard her saying to her friends, 'Oh this unsophisticated middle class!'

By then Mandira had brought the waiter who was now busy cleaning up.

'Okay, come, let's admire this whole scene as an abstract painting,' said Zafar.

'No, like an unsung song let's bind it with rhythm and then praise it.' Mihir gave me that strange glance again.

'Please Mihir, how's that possible? You people are half mad,' said Vandana, piqued.

'It's possible, Vandana ji.' Dr Sandeep handed me another glass of sherry.

'Because looking at something from different perspectives is what the life of an artist or a writer is about.' Mihir had stepped close to me again.

'You guys are beyond me,' said Vandana with her hand on her forehead.

What about the layers of make up on Vandana's face? It was equally mystifying. And it had started coming off with the sweat. Besides, the barbs by Pooja's mother still echoed in the room, adding to the negativity. She stood dressed in expensive clothes and obviously used an expensive perfume, like the other rich and famous people standing around. And amongst them stood I. In such a situation. As if bitten by a venomous reptile.

The waiter's towel had soaked all the bloody liquid.

Dr Sandeep was saying, 'Try and understand...because this is the difference that matters. The flow of blood in humans and machines tied together restores man's heartbeat; reconstructs him and the characters themselves.'

'Maybe. This is what you project.'

'And Mihir, this is Natasha, the famous dietician of our hospital, but she also has a doctorate in Psychology, which occupies her mind more. Her articles keep appearing in newspapers. You may have read them,' said Mandira, putting her arms around me.

'Oh, so I will have to make friends with her.' He gave me his gloved hand.

'Cheers, Mihir.'

'Cheers.' I put my trembling hand on his.

That day, when I was leaving the house, Vidyawati ji said, 'Beta, it's *shraadh* these days. There's food on a *thali* on the table. You don't believe in any of these festivals, but just touch that plate with your hands, put your palms together in respect, and I'll take it to the temple in Shailendra's name. It is his *shraadh* today. It's been two years he left and went away from out life.' She cried.

On the table there was a plate with *poori, sabzi* and *halwa* . As she had said I brought my palms together and bowed. 'Shailendra, wherever you may be, accept my love. You gave me limitless love which still lights me up from within. Maybe that's why I have no yearning left for anything. I am complete by myself and content, and can spend the rest of my life like that.'

As I reached the hospital, instead of taking the lift to the floor above I walked over to the room where Shailendra had breathed his last. The corridor looked familiar and embraced me and so did the bench where I had spent the most difficult year of my life. That bench was the sole witness to my occasional tears, my efforts at composure and hours of work I put into my research, making notes. Not only that, but I learnt so much here—humility, submission, arrogance, false dreams. Life wasn't life but a threadbare sheet falling apart, which could cover no worldly rites or rituals. It was Shailedra's suffering, but my responsibility. How much I had grown in a year. Responsibility had plucked me out of my immature, carefree life and made me conscious of larger issues. I had matured. I had even forgotten to laugh. That's why I feel that the whole of creation is pointless. Why does the sun rise? Why does the moon? Why do the planets exist? The dying Shailendra on this bed, in this room had blocked all the possibilities in my life. Why?

Just then someone shook my shoulder hard and said, 'Hello madam. Can you help me?'

Snapping out of my thoughts I saw a young, good looking man with an impressive personality with a delicate looking woman whom he held carefully in his arms. It seemed as though a gust of fresh air had paused.

'Yes, tell me. How can I help you?' I got up and tried to help him with the woman. 'Oh, she's unconscious.'

'Yes. That's why I brought her here. Please get her admitted.' He seemed to be in a hurry.

'Okay.' I ran down and brought Sister Dorothy. She took her to the room in front, Shailendra's room, and made her lie on his bed. Quickly she put the oxygen mask on her face. Dr Sandeep arrived and began to examine her.

The young man came and stood next to me. I wanted to take leave from the scene and head to my clinic. But before I could turn around he blocked my path. 'How can I thank you? You've helped me so much—oh, of course I know you—I met you at some party. Do you remember...

Mihir Sarkar? What a coincidence. What are you doing here?'

'I'm a dietician in this hospital.' I tried my best to prevent my voice from shaking.

'Oh. Good that I ran into you. Let me hand over her purse and passport to you.I don't know anybody in this city. Zafar's my friend and I just accompanied him to the party.'

'But this woman—who is she? Is she related to you?'

'Oh no, she isn't related to me at all. She is a traveller. When I was coming from London I offered her a lift in my taxi. We travelled together from the airport. She wanted to see the Taj Mahal before checking into the hotel. She was in a rush.'

'You didn't know this woman from Adam and still you invited her? And Mihir ji...we just met a fortnight ago at that party. How did you land up in London?'

'There was a literary commitment—a seminar. I keep going abroad now and then. Tomorrow I have to reach Jaipur. The literary festival is about to begin.'

'And this woman? Is she a writer like you?'

'No no...she told me she's a well-known fashion designer. She works for a branded company in London. She's quite senior in her field. I was quite impressed by her mannerisms and sophistication; we become friends during the few hours of the journey. I thought I'd talk to her, get to know her better. We need such characters for our novels, you see.'

'Oh I see.' My mind was suddenly filled with fog.

'When we started from Delhi she was absolutely fine. I don't know what happened when we reached the Taj Mahal. She was talking to the guide when suddenly she sat down on a platform and closed her eyes. Slowly she turned numb. The guide was quite helpful. He brought her water and the first-aid but by then she lost consciousness. The guide said she should be taken to the hospital. The guide brought us here otherwise I am not aware of the city.

'But her treatment? Care? Who will do all that?'

'See...her purse has money in pounds and her credit card. Please deposit whatever you need to. I don't know much... about the hospital procedures.'

'That's fine...but who will take the responsibility? What if something happens?' I was scared. She was lying on Shailendra's bed.

'I really don't know. What needs to be done...whether she has a relative here...I have no idea. What should we do?'

'But you've signed all the documents, Mihir ji. Then?'

'Please act according to whatever is legal. I only helped her out of kindness as a co-traveller. I didn't even want to visit the Taj Mahal. But I just went along on an impulse. The irony is that I have a flight to catch to Jaipur, otherwise I would have stayed. I will have to leave. But you can take my mobile number. Oh, I didn't even ask you your name. Please do give me your number too.' He took out his mobile phone.

'I'm Natasha Mehra.'

'Oh.' He was startled. 'Look at this, Natasha.' He took her passport from me and opened it. 'She is Romi Mehra.' Place of birth, Agra, UP, India. What a coincidence! I find such incidents amazing.' His eyes looked troubled. 'So may I take your leave. Please take the purse and the passport. Strange. Neither of us is related to her and yet God has chosen us to look after her.'

I was in a dilemma. What should I do? How could I take the responsibility of a stranger? But she was Romi Mehra, a famous fashion designer. I was getting more nervous every moment.

Suddenly he turned around and said, 'Remember, Natasha ji, at that party we were arguing about computers and human emotions? Today the computer will help you. Please switch on a computer and Google her identity. She is quite a renowned fashion designer in the high circles of London. Throughout our taxi ride she was listing the names of the rich and famous people she has worked for. Her success story is also quite interesting.' From an Agra *gali* to London. From rags to riches.'

He was standing very close to me. For the first time I realized he was quite handsome. I could feel his breath on my neck, close enough to make me uncomfortable. While I waited for some inspiration to help me speak up, he picked up an iPad from the woman's belongings. 'Now, Natasha, go to Google and it will show you her details.'

For a while we stood in silence, bewildered by each other's circumstances.

'Okay.' I took the iPad, observing the figure who lay between us, between two strangers. Her eyes were closed and her face looked angelic and serene. God knows in what kind of a world she was wandering.

'Just look. You may spot some relative or friend, some address, something. Sorry about leaving you in this strange mess.' There was deep concern in his expressive eyes. 'I really don't know how this happened. Sometimes life manipulates you.'

As I touched the dark screen of the iPad, it started filling up with some black and white circles, enough to confuse me even more.

'Can I go? Otherwise I'll miss my flight. Let me leave now.' He gave me his gloved hand. 'I will call you whenever I can...'The sincerity in his voice was reassuring.

There was strange stillness in the room after he left.

I thought about what the little white circle moving on the computer screen meant? Was it virtual time or a summary of old times? What was it?